BLAZE

A BROKEN HORN RANCH NOVEL

R.M. NEILL

CONTENTS

Before You Begin ... VII

1. Blaze ... 1

2. Blaze ... 5

3. River ... 11

4. Blaze ... 17

5. River ... 22

6. Blaze ... 27

7. River ... 36

8. Blaze ... 44

9. River ... 53

10. Blaze ... 61

11. River ... 72

12. Blaze ... 79

13. River ... 87

14. Blaze ... 95

15. River ... 105

16. Blaze   116

17. River   124

18. Blaze   132

19. River   138

20. Blaze   148

21. River   157

22. Blaze   166

23. River   174

24. Blaze   183

25. River   191

26. Blaze   202

27. River   211

28. Blaze   221

Epilogue   227

Acknowledgments   233

Also By   235

Before You Begin

If you're familiar with my work, you'll know I like to keep things light.

But sometimes there's a bit of shadow skirting before we find the light.

This book mentions a topic that may be sensitive to some.

River will often mention how he cared for his mother when she was sick and later died. Blaze also shares how his mother died.

There is no in depth on page description of these deaths, only memories.

If the mention of caring for aging parents or the passing of a parent is a tender topic, please know it's mentioned in this book.

CHAPTER 1

BLAZE

"I guess this is it, huh?"

Heather's broken voice and trembling chin cause my eyes to water with unshed tears.

"Yeah." My voice cracks as I open my arms for her.

"I'm going to miss you." She whispers against my chest.

"We'll keep in touch. You're one of my best friends, Heather. I won't be out of your life for good. Just day to day. Think of how much you'll get done without me pesterin' you every three minutes."

She laughs softly and eases out of my arms. Wiping at her tears, she nods. "Maybe I'll get to go to the bathroom without you demanding something the minute I leave."

Heather forces a smile and I know she'll have a rough time adjusting, but she has a family to cushion the change. She's been my assistant since the first day I dared to chase a dream. From the day I opened our office in a single room next to a pizza place downtown and we always smelled like tomato sauce and garlic. Try as we might, we could never get the smell out of our clothes.

After I landed my first client, we moved up and rented two offices in a business district. We were stuck between a shipping company and a candle making place, but at least we didn't smell like pizza all the time. The two of us have weathered many storms. Without her support, I'd not be where I am today.

"I can still text you every day at 10:15, just in case."

"I just can't believe this day is here, Blaze. I guess I just thought we'd always work together. It's... weird."

Puffing out a breath, I sit in my office chair one last time. Deciding to sell my company and walk away from all this was a difficult choice. It was everything I'd ever dreamed of having. A massive multi-million dollar company with an entire suite of offices overlooking the lake and the most beautiful and affluent portion of Rosevale. The view itself is worth the money to buy the entire building.

But there's an emptiness in me. As more years passed, I found myself increasingly discontent with my achievements. My heart wasn't in it anymore and I don't know why. Well, that's not entirely true. I have an idea why. Being lied to by both lovers and people who I called friends is one reason. Being cheated on is another. My heart is more bruised and battered than I'm comfortable to admit.

Turns out when there are only dollar signs to look forward to every day, it's not the needed motivation to keep showing up. Money isn't what will put me back together again.

Heather thinks I'm just burned out. I've done too much too fast, and it's finally caught up to me. She might be right, but I think it might be more than that. Something a bit more personal. I need to remember where I came from. What I couldn't wait to leave behind because it was embarrassing then. But a return to a simpler life might help me find answers and settle this feeling in my chest I can't seem to find a name for.

"I know. It's gonna feel strange for both of us. But you won't be completely rid of me. You're still managin' my condo. I can't thank you enough for that."

She huffs a laugh and sits in the chair opposite me.

"You pay me. That's thanks enough."

We spend a quiet moment together in our usual morning positions. Fifteen years of working side by side, we worked better than most business teams. Better than some married couples. Heather is the one constant in my life I can always depend on. Well, her and my best friend Dan.

"Blaze?"

I must have zoned out again, and I raise my eyes to meet her watery ones. "I wouldn't mind a 10:15 text, you know."

Smiling, I swipe a stray tear from my cheek. "Done."

When her cell rings, and it's her daughter, she excuses herself to take it. Teenage drama, no doubt. I had my share of that growing up. It's not a time I'd like to return to either. Kids are cruel when you're different.

The sale of my company completed months ago. All the papers are signed, approved and filed, with tomorrow being the official first day of the new ownership. Tomorrow, I'm no longer the CEO and owner of BP Payex Industries.

No more power suits and fake dates.

No more board meetings and investor lunches.

And no more wondering if I trusted the right person.

I'm done with business, Blaze.

Instead, I'll be Blaze Porter, ranch hand on my best friend's rescue ranch. I'm already a silent partner. Dan runs the show well, but it's time for me to return to the country. Every visit to Dan's ranch over the years has lightened my heart in ways I don't always understand. It's the right place for me to find what I'm searching for. Even though I'm not entirely sure what it is I need.

The city life beckoned me all those years ago and, like the siren it is, I fell under its spell.

I wanted nothing more than to leave my old life behind. To become someone important and respected. By doing so, I lost a part of myself. It took me fifteen years to realize it, though. I'm a smart guy, but sometimes I'm slow to put the pieces together. But better late than never, right?

"Blaze, are you ready?"

With a last sweep of my office, I flick off the light and close the door. Heather waits at her desk for me.

"I don't know. But I sure hope so."

Arm in arm, we leave the quiet building. Staff went home hours ago and when we step onto the sidewalk, the warm glow of the building sign, BP Industries, lights up the sidewalk. Heather squeezes my arm and together we walk the block to my condo where she has a parking spot. A job perk for her since I don't own a vehicle. Parking downtown is expensive as hell and I won't tell her it's part of the reason I'm not selling my condo. I know she loves parking here. Sometimes it's the little things that bring us happiness.

"Take care, sweetheart."

We hug one more time and Heather, bless her heart, gets into her car without another word. I know she's barely holding on. But she'll be okay.

We both will.

Here's to a new beginning in an old life.

CHAPTER 2

BLAZE

Moving sucks.

The boxes and the paper. All the fucking moving stickers on your shit. It's annoying. Or maybe it's just me. It could honestly be either at this point.

First thing I found and unpacked was my coffee maker. Without the magic elixir to wade through all the boxes, (honestly, how do I have so much stuff?) I'm liable to light a match and run away from it all. Although if I do that, Dan won't be able to find me and I have to admit I'd miss him.

In fact, he's supposed to be here soon. Only my best friend would show up with breakfast for me before I've had my first coffee. But I overlooked the fact my fridge wouldn't have food in it yet and I'm no longer living in the heart of a city. Running over to the cafe across from my condo at odd hours of the day because I forgot to buy groceries is no longer an option.

Not only have I left the city, but most of the convenience of it, too. It seems small towns don't always have delivery services, hence my call to Dan for breakfast. Although, once I get unpacked and in a routine, I'll get used to it. I thrive on routine, but like, after coffee. And food.

"Hey, I have food. Don't attack."

Dan simply lets himself in my front door. No knocking needed. Especially out here in the country. I may have left twenty years ago, but it's still the standard to open the door and announce your presence instead of knocking. It's just the way it's always been in Bloomburg. If you walk in and I'm not wearing pants, that's your fault, not mine.

"You're a lifesaver. What did you bring?"

Dan cocks his head, looking at all the boxes piled around the house.

"How did you get so much stuff?"

"That's what I said! It seems you accumulate as you age. I bet I have more tupperware containers than any single man has any right to own." I point to a stack of boxes in the kitchen. "The movers labeled all of those as kitchen storage. I don't even know how I had room for them in my last kitchen."

Dan sets down our breakfast and, bless his heart, it's one of those thermal bags to fit over casserole dishes. He cooked for me.

"I have scrambled eggs, bacon, and pancakes. There should be enough there to tide you over until you go for groceries."

Reaching in his pocket, he hands me a sandwich bag with four pieces of squished bread. "I didn't toast them because then they'd be all soggy. We can use the oven if you haven't found the toaster."

He pulls a few packs of sugar from his pocket with the McDonalds logo on them.

"I found those in my glove box. Figured you didn't have any handy."

"If you didn't already give your heart to Martin, I'd be after it. You're the best friend ever."

Waving his hand, he brushes me off and unpacks the dish of food while I root around for my toaster.

"Yeah, yeah. You can stop kissing my ass. I'll always be here for you, no extra compliments needed." He frowns. "Shit. Have you found your plates and cutlery?"

"I did this mornin'. That's when I remembered I had no food and called you." I slide two plates over with forks and he plates the food. While he does, I get stuck in this kind of surreal moment. I've been here to visit Dan occasionally since I left and it's always been at his place. He's like a brother I never had and a best friend all in one. In the city, I missed him often. He put up with all my rambling calls when I didn't want to admit I was homesick and just wanted to hear him talk.

And when I called him in tears after I found out my ex not only cheated on me but had been stealing from me, he was there, too. But it's always been on the phone and now he's here. In my kitchen. My new permanent kitchen and it's so strange.

Dan passes me a plate with a raised brow. "What are you looking at me like that for?"

"You're in my kitchen. Like, I own this place and you can be here whenever. It's so... bizarre."

He grins as he puts the bread under the broiler. I gave up on finding the toaster. It's the whole food and coffee before functioning thing.

"It is a bit. I'm not gonna lie. I'm thrilled to have you back."

Rooting through another box, I hand him a pair of tongs to flip the bread.

"I'm just happy you're okay with me crashin' the ranch set up. I've been thinkin' about how much fun we used to have on the horses. Remember when we rode bareback that one day back to the ponds and when we got back on the horses after swimmin' yours tried to rub you off?"

He barks a laugh. "Oh god. That was Champ. That horse didn't like being wet. At all." He tosses the slightly brown toast on the counter. "That was a great day, though."

Sliding him a coffee, I nod in agreement.

"It was. And I think I made the right choice comin' back. It's a change, but I think I'm ready for somethin' different. As much as I feel like I ran away from somethin', I think I should be here. The ranch has always grounded me, you know."

As we eat our dry toast and lukewarm food, friendly silence surrounds us. Dan knows how I am. He knows everything about me.

"Not every guy is like Ted, you know. I know he did you dirty, but someone is out there who knows just what a gem of a human you are."

"I know. I'm gettin' better. Hell, it's been two years since that whole fuck up, but he sorta did me a favour?"

I've been thinking about it a lot. While he ripped my heart into tiny pieces and put my confidence through the shredder, it was a wake up call. A real call to take stock of my life. I achieved what I initially set out to do. I overachieved to be fair. I became a fucking billionaire. Initially, going to the city was to have the opportunity I couldn't have here. The school, the business contacts, even the setting to hold meetings. I had to go if I wanted to win the clients and build a company.

I was leaving the comfort of Dan's family and friendship to do it, though. But I had to prove I was more than the back country redneck most people assumed I was just because I talked funny. I made an error in judgement along the way with Ted.

Chewing on my bacon, I point my half-eaten piece at Dan. "Because he woke me up and made me see there's more to life than makin' money and wearin' fancy suits. And yes, not every guy will be like him. He's like the reverse lottery. There's no way I'll meet another one that bad. But with that wake up comes a lot of new feelins' and shit."

"You're so poetic."

"I wanna be back with the animals. Be outside. Use my hands for that simple stuff I usually pay someone for."

"Like make your breakfast?" He says dryly.

"I love you for makin' me breakfast, and I can cook once I have food." I finish eating my bacon pointer as Dan smiles at my rant. "The point is, I'm ready to enjoy my life. Experience the hell out of it. Now, if I find someone worthy along the way to do that with, well, yay me."

"I'll always support you. You know that." He drains his coffee with a grin. "And just because you're my business partner doesn't mean I'll go easy on the tasks for you. I'm putting you on sheep duty with a few of the other guys. It'll get you back on a horse too."

"Oh, is Joker still here? Can I take him?"

Dan laughs. "You're the only one he likes, so of course he's yours."

Joker was one of the first rescues Dan took in. Before the ranch was officially a rescue ranch and still primarily a working farm. Joker was the most beautiful quarter horse I'd ever laid eyes on. He was jet black with a single white patch around his right eye. The previous owners had left him to starve, and he was such a bag of bones when he came to the ranch. With a lot of love and patience, he trusted people again and for whatever reason; it was me he was drawn to. Maybe it's because I slept in the barn with him the first few nights he was here. I've told no one I did that, but I felt his fear like it was mine. My heart wouldn't let him be alone.

Joker's history was too close to my own.

Although he was pissed at me when we had him gelded. Like I was to be the protector of his balls and I'd let him down. Man, he gave me so much grief after that. He started nipping at me and pushing me into the boards with his butt. But he let me ride him and he behaved as soon as he saw the saddle. I like to think it's because he can't forget I talked to him all night until he settled and when he woke up, I was there to calm him all over again. He was definitely mine.

"So, two more days for you to get unpacked and then you can start. Sound good?"

"Sooner is better, so sure. Wednesday at what? 8 A.M?"

He snorts. "You're not getting off that easy. See you at 6 A.M. I'll have coffee."

"Damn. That's harsh. Good thing the commute is short."

We chat a bit more about how the ranch is going and how well he and Martin are doing. I love seeing my friend in love and how his body transforms just speaking about the man he fell hard for. It even makes me believe that one day I'll let someone back into my life, too.

Maybe.

Dan sees himself out and I continue the unpleasant task of unpacking.

Unpacking sucks.

CHAPTER 3

RIVER

"Hey Dan!"

Waving to my boss, I bounce up his front steps to grab a refill of coffee in the kitchen before work starts. He makes the best coffee. One day I'll ask how he does it.

"Thanks for coming over early. I wanted to introduce you properly to Blaze, since he's going to work with you for the next few months."

Dan mentioned his friend Blaze was also a partner in the ranch. He was coming back to work here now that whatever he used to do seemed to be over. I knew he'd come by a few weeks here and there to visit Dan before, but I always seemed to miss him. Dan never said a bad word about him. I wasn't concerned even a little about meeting the guy. But I appreciate the proper introduction.

Hell, any friend of Dan's is endorsement enough for me because Dan is one of the best people I know.

"Sure thing, Dan. I'm positive we'll get along just fine. You know me. I'm as laid back as they come."

"You sure are." He chuckles and runs a hand through his hair. "Listen, River, before he shows up, just... he's my best friend and... " Dan scratches his head and puffs out a breath. "He's a good guy."

"Uh, I assumed he would be. He's your friend, and he owns the ranch, too. I mean, other than just an introduction, I don't expect there to be any drama. Unless you're not telling me something."

Dan's eyes are soft as he speaks of his friend. There's a genuine tenderness there. While Dan has a heart of gold for everyone on this ranch, I think there's more to it with Blaze.

"No, I just worry about him sometimes."

"Ah, so you want me to report back if I notice anything?"

Dan's smile wavers, and he shakes his head. "Here he comes."

Now I knew we were going out on horses today. In fact, I wore my chaps today because I expected we'd do a bit of work in the high brush. Those thistles are nasty this time of year. But nothing, and I mean nothing, would prepare me for the vision crossing the yard towards me right now. You know when you take a bite of something that tastes so good; you take that extra moment to savour it for a little longer after it's already slid down your throat?

Yeah, that's how I feel seeing Blaze for the first time.

I stared a little too long, but honestly, how could I not? First, he's riding the most gorgeous black quarter horse you've ever seen, Joker. Joker has the right horse attitude needed to carry a man like Blaze, because just like the horse, Blaze commands your attention. Dark hair peeks out under his cowboy hat and a dark black well-trimmed beard covers his chin and extends up his jawline in a chinstrap pattern. Aviator sunglasses hide his eyes for now, but his smile could light up the darkest fucking night. His hands grip the reins with confidence and when he arrives at the house, he dismounts so smoothly you'd think he's been riding horses his whole life. Of course, maybe he had. I only know he's here after years in the city.

But like savouring the taste of the most amazing thing you've ever had in your mouth, I should have snapped my mouth shut then and said hello. But I didn't. Because those designer jeans hugged him in all the right places and it was hard, physically hard, to tear my eyes away. I've truly never seen a man like Blaze in person and it makes my heart thump an extra thump and my mouth go dry. It's not until Dan gives me a little nudge that I swallow and say hello.

"You must be Blaze. I'm River. Nice to meet you."

Oh god, I sound like a boy whose voice just broke with puberty.

Blaze takes my offered hand, model smile still tacked in place and again, turns all my cranks with his damn accent.

"Mornin', nice to meet ya."

His country drawl with the dropped letters and the way his smile is part of every word kinda knocks me for a loop.

"Um, you too."

Ugh. Smooth.

Thankfully, Blaze just lets that pass and Dan says he has coffee ready, which draws Blaze into the house, giving me a few moments to get my shit together. Which is good because I'm all kinds of rattled and we have to work together? This might become the worst job ever if I can't concentrate.

Well, I guess I should be happy there's more than just green scenery and sheep to watch all day.

A bit of sweet eye candy to break up the day can only make the days pass faster, right?

Wrong.

So much wrong.

After Blaze filled a travel mug of coffee and remounted his horse, I met up with him on my horse, Sly. Sly is a laid back mare who has a bad habit of escaping from her stall and walking up to Dan's front door. Some days, a horse snout greets Dan at his kitchen window. Other days, it's a horse grazing in his front yard. But it was a long way from where Sly came from. She had spent her whole life in a small barn and only saw people when they threw food in and remembered to feed her. Why she didn't develop her escape tendencies then, I'm not sure. I like to think it's because she finally learned what it was like to be loved and she just wanted to be with people all the time.

And it's her curiosity to meet new people that is about to make life interesting.

I want her to walk beside Blaze so we can talk and get to know each other, but she keeps veering into Blaze and Joker making our legs brush together.

"Sly, would you save the curiosity for when the man is off his horse, please?"

Blaze laughs, and it's warm and happy. Like a hug.

"I heard about Sly, but we never really met. She likes people, right?"

"Yeah, that's her. A real people person. Sometimes I can't just control her, you know? Sorry for the bumping."

"It's okay. I sort of understand. She just wants to be with the ones who gave her freedom and made her happy." He drinks from his pink glittery travel mug and I hide my smile.

"Is that why you've come to the ranch? Freedom and happiness?"

Maybe that's too much to ask right away, but his words make mine tumble from my lips without a second thought.

He shrugs a shoulder and reaches over to scratch Sly's ears when she swings her head over again. "Somethin' like that. One person's prison is another's idea of freedom, right? Happiness is subjective. Sly, I imagin' sees happiness as somethin' like this ear scratch. I think I need somethin' a little more than that. I just don't know what it is yet?"

Blaze leaves his words hanging, and I wonder what his real issue is. But his melting smile tells me he's not uncomfortable with my questions and I breathe an internal sigh of relief. I don't want to make him uncomfortable, but I want to get to know him.

Sly can't help herself and throws her head at his shoulder again, lurching me half off the saddle.

"Oof. God, Sly, you're killing me."

Joker whinnies, unimpressed by her display, but Blaze pats him on the neck. "It's okay, boy. You're still my favourite. Sly just wants to make friends. So be nice."

Blaze pushes her gently away and I pull Sly back, giving her a nudge to get in front.

One thing about Sly, she may love people, but she also loves to run.

"I'll see you up there!"

I toss the words over my shoulder and give Sly all the slack to take us away. The wind in my face as she gains speed is always a thrill to me, and laughter boils over as I lean low into her neck. The world melts away as fast as her hooves pound the ground and, for this moment in time, when we run in the morning, I can take on the world.

Chapter 4

Blaze

River, I've noticed, is mainly quiet and keeps to himself. Except for the first day we met, he keeps his conversation to morning hellos and the tasks at hand. When it's time for breaks, he takes the food that's brought out by a ranch hand with a thank you and a warm smile. But he rarely stays to talk with me. Not the case with the other ranch hands, though.

The other men on the ranch display a deep respect for him. They seek him out for advice on more than just work related things from what I can tell and I've yet to see him ever not make time for one of them. While the people seeking me out were sometimes false in their motives in the business world, these men openly adore River. There's no ulterior motive. He seems to be a genuinely good guy. With a unique hobby.

River likes to whittle.

Spring has truly sprung and we've been monitoring the pregnant ewes and newborn lambs more closely. In the weeks he's been across the meadow from me, I've been watching him work with a piece of wood and a knife. His brow furrows and his pink tongue darts out to lick his lips as he continuously shapes a block of wood into something recognizable. I've always admired anyone with artistic abilities. I was born with an analytic brain. It's great for business, but not so much for finding a relaxing outlet.

Sly stands still if he's seated on her, too. That fascinates me. This people loving horse, who always likes to cause trouble with her nose and escaping, adores River just as much as the ranch hands. It's like she knows it's not the time to joke around when he's in his zone. The bond between an animal and a human tells you more about the human than the animal.

He'll monitor his side of the fence before flicking his glance my way. If he catches me watching, he has this shy, boyish smile he shoots me before ducking his head back to his project. I think I'm obsessed with that smile.

"Hey Blaze!"

My hand lurches, spilling my cold coffee into my crotch.

"Jesus, Heath! You scared the shit out of me. Next time, make some noise."

He cocks his head and thumbs over his shoulder.

"I did? I came up on the quad with coffee, hot chocolate and sandwiches for you and the boys. You should've heard me coming a mile away."

Huh. I always hear him coming.

"Oh, right."

I whistle two sharp blasts, signalling to the others we have a food break.

"How much longer will you guys be out here with the sheep?"

"Few more weeks, I think. There are still more ewes due yet. Once they're done, we have a few new ranch hands and we'll start the sheep herd control."

"Dan said I could help! What do I get to do for the herd stuff?"

"I think we'll see what you're good at first and go from there."

Heath sets our beverages and snacks on a table near a storage building. Dan has given him this task as a step up from mucking stalls. He seems like a good kid trying to find his way in life. Nobody has been more eager than him every day to get here and help. I, for one, appreciate his enthusiasm.

As he sets up the food, he knocks the hot beverage carafe over and barely saves the sandwiches he just placed out.

His work ethic is top-notch. His clumsiness is frightening.

"Hooo, boy that was close, eh, Blaze? We almost had to have mushy sandwiches."

"Hi, Heath. You're still our caterer? I thought you were helping us with the sheep?"

River joins us first, and he nods a hello my way before taking a sandwich off the table and leaning against the wall to unwrap it.

"Yeah! Dan says I can start soon. Maybe Monday, but he wanted to check with Blaze."

Both pairs of eyes turn to me and for the first time since I've been here, I allow myself to stare at River close up. His jaw works as he chews and he's so relaxed. Leaning against the wall of the shelter, booted ankles crossed, he projects an easy confidence. And he's not hard to look at. Little bits of yellow fleck his warm brown eyes and even smiling with a mouthful of food, there's this little laugh line that pops out on his cheek. It's deeper than the others, but not quite a dimple.

That pink tongue darts out to lick the corner of his mouth, and I focus on his soft lips. I wouldn't be opposed to finding out what he tastes like. I wonder if his lips are as soft as they look?

Maybe I've stared too long or maybe he can read my mind because he clears his throat and raises an eyebrow.

"So Blaze, what do you think? Can he start Monday? I think we could use his help and ease him into it."

River's voice is light as he turns his attention to Heath and I have to shake the fog from my head. Jesus, I just zoned out, staring at the man.

"Uh, yeah. I think we can work you into it on Monday, Heath. We can start you with somethin' easy to get the hang of it."

Heath gives a whoop and pumps the air with his fist. "Awesome! Not that I don't enjoy bringing you all food every day, but I want to try other things. I'm ready." With pressed lips, he nods his head and I have to smile at his youthful exuberance.

"Then we'll make it so. I'll talk to Dan tonight."

Heath bounces about in happiness and trips over his own feet, causing him to stumble into the wall.

"Whoopsie. Got a bit too carried away there."

River chuckles in his space and gazes at Heath with a fondness I can't quite place. "Enthusiasm is a good thing, Heath. We just need you to make sure you don't hurt yourself."

When the other ranch hands show up, I slip out of the space and around the corner when the conversation turns to their families. I know Heath doesn't have one, but hearing River and Reed talk about their parents makes my chest ache.

I prefer to disappear before they send questions to me about family. It's the polite thing to do to include me, but I don't like to talk about it, even with a group of men who are as great as these guys seem to be.

If there's one thing I've noticed other than River since coming here, it's the deep family like bonds most of the guys seem to share. It shouldn't surprise me. It was the one thing Dan strived to do with the people on the ranch and with each visit, I noticed how he's grown his own little odd collection of family, one person at a time. Dan wants no one to feel left out or unloved, and he loves these guys. I see it in his actions towards them every day, and having known him for twenty-five years, I know how his affection can change a person's life.

As their conversation drifts out of the shelter, it's a reminder to me that this is more than a ranch with animals to care for.

We're here to take care of each other, too.

And I don't know if I'm ready for that yet.

CHAPTER 5

RIVER

"You good with the gate, Heath?"

He gives me a thumbs up as I wrangle the little lamb in my arms. This one is smaller than the others and I place her on the scale before we tag her and vaccinate.

We started our herd control inventory a week ago, but I missed out. I'm trying to do double duty today to make up for them being short handed that long. Seeing Blaze after a week away was like finally getting that cold drink at the end of a long, hot day. He had become part of my daily routine and even though I still didn't know him; I missed him. Which was strange.

After the second day at my dad's bedside, Blaze had sent me a text. It wasn't anything special, I'm sure, but the gesture touched me. He simply wished my dad a speedy recovery and urged me to take the time needed for him. But there was something about that simple message that sat more firmly in my heart than it should have.

The mother sheep who already had her once over paces outside the gate waiting for her baby.

"Female. Twenty-seven point six pounds and no special markings." I run my hand under her belly as she bleats. "No evidence of hernia."

Blaze punches it all into a hand-held device to store the herd info. Next, he attaches it to a tag number he pulls out of the bin and readies the tagging gun. With a quick pinch, she barely flinches, and he draws the vaccine into the syringe with his large, capable hands. Blaze is only an inch taller than me, but his hands seem like the size of frisbees compared to mine. But those hands are always gentle on the animals. Even the ornery ones. I wonder how they'd feel on me?

He tents the lamb's skin to deliver the vaccine and my mind wanders off to places it really shouldn't when there's a pointy thing around. When the lamb lurches, there's a sharp, burning pain in the meat of my thumb and a curse leaves my lips as I draw my hand to my chest.

"Shit! Don't let her out, Heath." Blaze yells before immediately rounding the table and pulling my hand from my chest.

"I'm so sorry, River. Are you okay?"

My voice is stronger than I thought it would be with his hands on me. The very hands I was just fantasizing about are touching me with a gentleness far beyond what I imagined.

"Um, yeah. I mean, it was my fault. I wasn't paying attention."

A pained hum from his throat has my gaze fly to his.

"It was my fault. I was the one not payin' attention."

There's a small trickle of blood on my hand where the needle went through and the surrounding skin is an angry red. A dull throb has set in the area, but it's not the end of the world.

"Do you want to go to the hospital?" He whispers, still with my hand in his and his rough fingertips softly stroke the inside of my palm.

"No. I don't think so. I'll just get the first aid kit —"

"No. I'll do it. Come with me." He guides me by the elbow to the gate out of the little pen. "Heath, secure the gate and help Reed vaccinate that lamb while I take care of River. Take a break and wait for us when that's done."

"You got it, boss!"

Blaze in charge mode is... fucking sexy. Even if it's because he's about to do some minor first aid on my hand.

Pulling the first aid kit from the ATV's supply box, he motions for me to sit down.

I say nothing more as he wipes the area with an alcohol swab and I hiss with the sting.

Leaning down, he gently blows air across the area and my whole body shivers. "Sometimes just a little air across the skin takes the sting away." He murmurs. He glances up under his dark eyelashes and he quickly looks away. "It used to work for me when my mom did it."

I don't know what to say. My tongue feels like a cement slab and I can't form words even if I wanted to. All I can do is watch as he dabs some ointment on the area and secures a large bandage over it.

"If you can take ibuprofen it would help with the swelling. I have some if you like?"

"Sure." I clear my throat when it comes out all scratchy and garbled. "I mean, sure, I can take it."

When he walks back to the sheep shelter for something to help me swallow the pill he hands me, I stare after him. Who is this gentle and fierce man who can blow on my wound to take the sting away one moment and then bark orders to the rest of the ranch hands the next?

Returning, he hands me his usual pink, glittery thermal mug with a shrug. "It's all that's left in there and I don't know where your thermos is."

"It's okay. I don't mind sharing your cup. You don't have cooties, do you?"

I'm hoping to lighten the mood with the childish word and it works.

Those full lips tick up in a smile, and he snorts. "The last I checked, I'm all clear and cootie free."

With the mood now back to something less charged, I decide to just go with it.

"I'm happy to hear that since your prick was in me."

His eyes widen and I don't miss the bob of his throat as he works to form words.

"I... uh.. " A flush of his cheeks makes me smile. He's embarrassed?

Blaze finally recovers and when his blue eyes crash into mine, the flash of heat wipes the teasing smile from my face.

"My prick doesn't poke things by accident. Only with purpose." He squeezes my arm lightly. "If you're okay to continue, we only have a few more to call it a day."

"I'm okay to help. With anything."

I don't take my eyes off him. Is there something there? Or am I misreading him completely?

With a nod, he steps away. "You can do the data entry while Reed and I finish up then."

Staring after his back, I'm even more intrigued by this man. But my gut tells me to step back.

Walking back to the pen, he's already returned to work mode, but now I know with certainty there's something underneath the surface of Blaze. A part of him he's keeping away from the rest of us.

It's a good thing I'm patient.

All good things come to those who wait.

CHAPTER 6

BLAZE

One Year Later

"So, how do you feel about chickens?" Dan asks.

"Uh, they taste good?"

Another sunny morning and another day that starts with coffee, my best friend and apparently, talk of chickens.

"I have another project, if you don't mind." Dan beams his signature smile.

"I'm sure I won't mind. What is it?" Taking the travel mug he hands me, I immediately take a sip. Perfection, as always. Dan brews the best coffee.

He motions for me to follow him across the ranch yard.

"I want to get the chicken coop built here." He points to the area Alec cleared in the spring. It's a decent sized patch of yard between Dan's main house and Alec's smaller house. "I arranged for the delivery of materials. They should be here this morning."

"Sounds good. You want me to build it, then?"

Since returning to the ranch from leaving my business life behind, I've loved being involved with all the projects. It reminds me of when we were kids and tried to build a wooden car for the Boy Scouts race. Dan failed epically on his own, but the two of us built a decent car together once. That was a lot of fun.

Dan nods, avoiding my gaze. "Yep. With Heath and River."

Cue the record scratch in my happy brain.

A weary sigh crosses my lips. "Heath has no business near power tools. You know this. He's a great guy, but I'll be playin' doctor every day and not the fun kind."

Dan at least has the decency to appear apologetic.

"I know, but he really wants to get into some kind of trade, and I promised I'd let him help you both."

I'm a patient man, but I'm not a saint. I like Heath, he's funny and a good kid. Well, he's not a kid anymore, but he's young. Dan took him in as a teenager when he was straight out of juvenile detention and scared as all hell to live life. He's great with manual labour and caring for the small animals. He can input data like nobody's business when we do any kind of animal tracking. One thing he cannot do, and I can't stress this enough, is make it through the day without hurting himself.

I groan. "Dan, I don't know. This feels like a bad idea."

"Since when have you ever turned down a challenge?" He drinks from his own mug as he turns to me. "River will help you. It's not just you."

"So why can't River just do it?"

Dan laughs. "Because he's too nice to everyone. I need your take no shit attitude for when Heath tries to do something on his own and he's not ready." He shakes his head. "Honestly, it's a chicken coop and a fence. It should take the three of you three days tops."

"You know, sometimes I don't understand why you're my best friend. This might drive me back to smokin'."

Dan laughs and punches me playfully in the arm.

"You're so melodramatic. Honestly, I need you to do this."

I don't know why he can't pick anyone else for this. Like his main ranch hand, for one.

"So I can't pull the rich guy card and just say no?"

"If I gave you the option, would you? Besides, you said you loved doing all the things with your hands."

With a sigh, I smile. "No, you're right. It's fine, I'll do it."

"Don't act like you aren't having fun." Turning towards me, he peers over the edge of the mug. "You've been here awhile now and you've had your hand in a lot of different things. Vaccinating sheep, training the draft horses, building stalls and now a chicken coop. I think this has been good for you, yes?"

Clearing my throat, I gaze off into the pasture where Alec has turned out the horses. I thought nothing could ever replace my love of the view of the lake in the city, but it has.

"Very good, Dan. I've lost ten pounds and gave up smokin'. I didn't think I missed the quiet, but... I think I did."

"Do you think you found what you were hoping for?"

Sipping my coffee, I shrug. "Sort of? I feel much more... grounded. I think that's how to describe it. Like this is where I should be now."

"But? It seems like there's more to that."

River's beat up pick-up truck comes rolling into the yard, followed closely by the delivery truck from Wood Mart. Dan waves the delivery over while River parks next to my white Ford F-150.

He heads our way with Dan's dog, Daisy, bouncing and circling him as he smiles down at her.

"Are we building something today?" He smiles and that not quite dimple thing pops up. It's hard not to smile back.

"Yep. A chicken coop and a fence. Dan already marked out the fence line. You, me and Heath."

"Ah, I guess that means Heath wants to try carpentry. That's cool."

River makes eye contact with me and we both laugh at the unspoken message. Heath will hurt himself. River and I have worked together enough with Heath the past year that we know this.

Dan smacks my shoulder, and I understand his hidden look. He'll be continuing our private conversation later. With a wave, he heads back to the house and leaves us to it.

"I'll have a first aid kit on hand, don't worry. But I'm very hesitant to have him operate anythin' with sharp blades and power."

River hums in agreement. "True, but he needs to try and learn. I can watch him when we get to that part. What are we doing until he gets here?"

The crew unloads the truck, and we stand watching. We could help, but I know River used to work for them and keeps his distance. He removes a small chunk of wood and a knife from the pocket of his flannel jacket. With expert hands, he works the piece of wood as we wait.

"How'd you get so good at that?" I ask.

Last year, when he helped with sheep, I'd often find him whittling or carving while sitting on his horse. He keeps a small knife hidden on him at all times. I'd eventually learned he liked to carve, and he was damn good at it. The custom counter for Colby's candy store he built is exquisite. He had also mentioned building furniture, which again I didn't see firsthand until his work for Colby.

River was a very talented artisan.

"Oh, ah, it's a bit of a story to tell." He huffs a laugh and I motion for him to tell it.

Since I jabbed him with the sheep vaccine last year and we shared what I call a very personal moment, I pulled away. I avoided any kind of deep conversation with him. It scared me when I thought about what could happen if I let him in. But over time, I've warmed up to the idea of maybe letting my guard down and learning to let someone be close to me again.

"We've got time."

Nodding, he focuses on the small block of wood and continues. "When I was thirteen, my mom was really sick. She spent a lot of time in bed and I kept her company sitting there. If she was awake, we talked, or I read to her from whatever book I was into. But when she was asleep, I carved. I tried it one day to focus on anything other than her being sick." He goes quiet for a moment and I'm mesmerized, watching him turn a square chunk of wood into something recognizable.

"One therapist I had told me to try a hobby to occupy my thoughts. I have to always be mindful about the sharp blade, so there was no time for me to think of mom and the future."

His hands are steady, and a glance at the block shows the start of a teddy bear. It's incredible.

"I'm sorry to ask such a personal question. I didn't know it had such meanin' to you."

"Oh, it's okay. I know most people think it's just a hobby or something I picked up and got good at. In a way it is, but there are a lot of therapeutic benefits to it. Which is why I keep doing it, I guess. I mean... I love doing it, but it keeps my mind occupied."

The workers signal they're done and River places the project back in his pocket with a smile. "I guess it's time for us to get started on this coop for Dan."

Together, we walk to the piles of materials and I peel off the plans for the coop. River separates the lumber, explaining it will help him teach Heath how to be efficient on a job site. I set up a makeshift table nearby with all the hardware for the project and follow River's lead with sorting.

When we're organized and ready to start the project, Heath still hasn't arrived. Since Dan requested we do it with him, neither of us wants to move ahead until he shows. We take a seat on the porch swing instead and wait for Heath.

River returns to his whittling and I send Heather my promised morning message a little early. Ever since I left the city, I still text her at the same time every morning. I initially thought we'd both fall away from it, but after a year, we still keep the habit and I think it's been a great help to both of us adjusting.

We share a brief text exchange and I laugh out loud when Heather includes a photo of her daughter Mikayla covered in mud but laughing because she misjudged a puddle on a nature walk. She tried to jump over and didn't make it.

"Mind if I ask who you talk to every morning?" River asks with a smile.

"Oh, my close friend Heather. She was my assistant for fifteen years. She just sent me a picture of her daughter."

I show it to River and he laughs.

"I'm impressed she's smiling. No teenager I've ever encountered would be happy about that."

"She's a good kid. Very laid back, like her mom. I'm sure she was a ball of rage for the first minute it happened, but then laughed it off."

Mikayla was probably more upset she ruined her clothes than being embarrassed over falling into a puddle.

"Um, so, I wanted to tell you something." River places his project down and shifts to look at me. "I'm so happy you stepped up to help Colby get his store back. I appreciated the opportunity to help, too. He's a good guy, you know. I don't have a lot of money, but I have a talent. I'm just really happy you included me." He smiles, a shy boyish smile. The same one I was developing an addiction to last year. "I just wanted to say thanks for that."

For a moment, I'm not sure how to respond. But River is sincere with his words and I should return the same to him. I should try to get to know him better.

"Uh, you're welcome. Thanks for tellin' me that. I was worried the guys here might think I was tryin' to snow them over, you know. I didn't tell anyone who I was because..."

"Because people are quick to judge and you wanted us to see you first, not money."

I blink at his open honesty. "That's exactly it. Yeah. Well, there's other stuff too, but that was a part of it. It's just not somethin' I ever feel comfortable bringin' up in conversation."

He nods. "I understand how you want to hide." He snorts. "Also explains how you accidentally vaccinated me last year. You were used to operating a stapler, not syringes."

"Hey!" I laugh, remembering my horror at having jabbed River in the hand with a sheep vaccine. He laughed it off, after a few curse words, of course, but we continued the day like it never happened.

I was beyond mortified about it. Especially since the reason it happened was because I was distracted that day. He'd returned to work after a week off and he let his beard grow. I couldn't stop thinking about how much more attractive he was with it.

And when I forced him to let me put a Band Aid on him and blew on it like he was some kid, it embarrassed me for showing a tender side. Even when he played along with me, I backed out of the situation. It was hard, but I wasn't ready.

"To be fair, I used to help Dan and his grandparents when we were kids. I was rusty, not green. There's a difference."

Even I can't keep the smile off my face now, so I turn to face River, enjoying this new banter we have going on.

"I'm here because truthfully, that way of life wasn't workin' for me anymore."

He tilts his head. "Sounds rather serious."

A loud car enters the yard and grinds to a halt in front of the farmhouse with a belch of exhaust. Heath exits from his lime green Pinto he must have salvaged from a scrap yard. There's more rust than green on the body and I'm certain he lost the muffler about twenty years ago.

"Hi guys!"

"You're late." I say.

"Sorry. There was a duck on the side of the road on the way here and I stopped."

"You stopped for a duck because...."

"Oh! Just because it was pretty. Then I kind of lost track of time, but here I am!"

No human can remain mad at another human simply because he's late for watching a duck. It's just not possible.

"Well, let's get started then. The three of us have a chicken coop to build, and we're teachin' you about carpentry."

"Yay! I love chickens."

As we walk to the material set up, Heath trips and stumbles into the side of the table with the hardware. Nails go flying and he pulls his hands away.

"Ouch, that's a huge splinter. Anybody have tweezers?"

With a sigh, I grab the first aid kit and throw a glance at River. He bites his lip, holding the laughter in and before I know it, I'm laughing too.

And it feels good.

CHAPTER 7

RIVER

Blaze is an interesting guy.

When we first met, he felt like he was an old friend I hadn't seen for a while. He was friendly but slightly withdrawn, like he didn't say everything all at once. But he wanted to. We worked well together. I admired the fuck out of how he could take charge when the situation needed it. Whether it was herding the sheep, working the drafts, or coming to the aid of a friend, he took over with the confidence of a man who was used to being at the helm of the ship.

He withdrew from me after the vaccine accident though, and I've always thought maybe it was because I flirted with him too soon. While not my boss, maybe it was inappropriate then, but he's hard not to like.

He's handsome, warm and funny. He's gentle.

And then we all find out he's a damn billionaire.

We knew Blaze and Dan were teenage best friends and we knew Blaze was a partner at The Broken Horn Ranch as well. That was all we knew when he arrived to work with us.

But when he showed up in a suit and I barely recognized him without his Stetson, learning there was a deeper layer to him wasn't a surprise. He always had a fancy phone with a stylus he'd text on or add notes to. He kept his scruff neatly trimmed and I'm almost positive he had to oil it or something because his beard was shiny as fuck. I bet it was soft, too. Not that my other coworkers were slobs who didn't practice good hygiene. There was just something different about Blaze. He stood out even when I could tell he didn't want to.

And that was something I couldn't quite figure out yet. Why did he seem open yet so guarded all at once?

Finding out he was the man who built the most practical online payment processor for businesses and captured the entire market in a mere seven years after launching was not what I thought he was hiding. But I could understand why he wouldn't want to broadcast that fact. I bet he had people trying to talk him out of money all the time.

But there was more than that.

I don't know why, but I have a feeling that's not the real reason he's here.

"I think we made good progress today." I say with what I hope sounds like confidence.

Surveying the results, we in fact, did not make good progress. Teaching Heath slows the process down far more than I expected. He's eager to learn, though, and it makes teaching him fun. He's as clumsy as a cat in snowshoes too. We'd barely started the measuring and cutting to build the walls when he somehow pinched his finger with the tape measure and made it bleed.

Blaze handled it well and after the second accident in two hours, he wisely left the first aid kit out on the table.

"We did, didn't we?" Heath is proud of our efforts so I'm not about to bring him down.

"How about you try to get here a little earlier tomorrow? We can make up for lost time?" I ask.

Blaze nods. "Good idea. If it takes a little longer than normal, that's fine, but I'd like to have it done by Friday."

"I can do that." Heath beams. "No stopping for ducks. Or turtles! I'll be here!"

Heath waves over his shoulder and Blaze and I watch as he hits his head getting into his car.

"How does that kid manage to not seriously maim himself every day?" Blaze shakes his head before gathering the tarps to cover up our materials.

"I imagine he has a lot of bruises on his body. And scars. Lots of scars. But he did great."

Making sure all the tools are back in the box, I place it under the tarp for Blaze and we strap it down. There's a chance of rain tonight, so we're protecting the supplies.

"You're a great teacher, River." Blaze removes his hat and aims a smile my way.

"Thanks. You are too."

He snorts. "Don't tell me lies. I have zero patience for teachin'. Unless it's readin' stock prices and financial reports, I find it hard to teach anyone anythin'. It's not one of my skills."

Laughing, I concede to his honesty. "Okay, you're right. I could tell when he got his finger stuck in the measuring tape, you weren't happy. But you did well. We make a good team. I make sure Heath stays in one piece and you keep the project moving."

He smiles again, and not for the first time, I notice how his eyes crinkle when he does. It's a good look on him.

"So, do you have any plans tonight?" Blaze asks.

We walk back to our vehicles and pause at the back of his pick-up. It's a lot nicer than mine, but Blaze has never flaunted he has money.

"Ah, no. I'm pretty boring. I'll probably do some carving in my shop or work on building a piece for the ranch's fund raiser. If I have time, I'll donate a custom address sign and something I already have made in my shop."

Blaze's eyes light up. "You have a workshop? That's super cool. Where is it?"

"Oh, it's actually a detached garage behind my house. Handy for those late nights when I can't sleep. I just go to the shop and carve or sometimes paint. It settles the mind."

That was a lot to spill out, but again, there's something about Blaze that keeps me talking. And I want him to know me. I want to know him. Badly.

"I need to find that, I think." He leans against his truck with his arms crossed. "Since I've been here, I've used the ranch to distract myself. I was a permanent fixture on Dan's couch for many nights. I think he and Martin would like more private time, so I've cut back on that."

If I'm not mistaken, there's a twinge of loneliness in Blaze's voice. In fact, I'm positive because I feel the same.

"Do you want to learn how to whittle?" I blurt before I have time to rethink it.

That smile shows up again and I grin like a fool since I put it there.

"You'd teach me? For real?"

"Yeah, of course. If I knew you were so interested, I would've offered a lot sooner." Which is true. Blaze has intrigued me since day one, but he didn't seem like he wanted to let anyone in. He was friendly, but it was through the screen door kind of friendly. He'd talk to you but never invite you inside. So I stood back and observed all things Blaze.

Grinning again, he opens the door to his truck.

"I'll send you a text. After dinner tonight, okay?"

"That's perfect."

Blaze drives off, leaving me standing next to his empty parking space. I don't notice Dan has sidled up next to me.

"How'd it go today, River? Heath keep all his fingers attached?"

I chuckle. "He did. He was great. I'm not sure if carpentry will be his thing or not yet, but we'll figure it out."

Dan's gaze feels heavy, so I turn to him.

"What's wrong?"

He smiles, slow and easy, as is Dan's way. "Nothing." He whistles to Daisy, and she trots back up to the farmhouse with him.

Before he opens the door, he turns back to me and winks.

Shaking my head, I hop into my truck and drive home.

After supper, my phone buzzes with a text from Blaze asking for my address, just like he said he would.

I reply and make sure he knows how to find my place before switching the outdoor lights on.

Now that it's confirmed, and he's on his way, I'm pacing the hallway and watching out the window every time I hear a vehicle. Which is silly. I invited him and he's coming over. He'll be in my most private of spaces in ten minutes.

And when I think of it like that, no wonder I'm hyperventilating.

I need a voice of reason that this isn't a bad thing to have Blaze here. I need my best friend, Kelly. She always knows what to say.

I put her on speakerphone as I peak out the window for the eightieth time.

"Hiya, River! What's shaking baby?"

Kelly is without a doubt the best friend I could ever ask for. The only real one I have left, too. She knows every single thing about me, just like I do about her. Talking to her always sets me straight. Well, not that kind of straight. That went out the window when I was twelve and I saw David Hasselhoff in a swimsuit. I moved solidly from questioning to confirmed that day.

Kelly was the first one I told and with her encouragement, I told my parents not long after. Mom and Dad, I knew, wouldn't turn me away for being gay. But so many stories float around about parents throwing out their kids, it made me doubt their acceptance. The stress and anxiety I already felt being the odd kid was now compounded by a label. But there was no way I could keep it all bottled up. I was never good at that, even after mom died. My stress in the end was all for nothing. They both hugged me and thanked me for trusting them. Mom then told me to make sure the lawn got mowed, or I'd have no allowance.

"I don't shake. I undulate." I say, laughing at our inside joke. We both think undulate is a sexy word and people should use it in normal conversation more often.

She snorts. "Ha ha. You stuck on a project tonight? Looking for advice? You don't normally call me on a weeknight."

"Sheesh, am I that predictable?"

"Only with phone calls, Riv. So what's up?"

"Remember the guy I work with I told you about, Blaze?"

"The cute guy with a great ass who came out as a billionaire?"

"Did I say he had a great ass?"

Legit question. It's not wrong. I just don't remember saying it.

"You did. I think it was when we had margaritas for my birthday and you started talking to the cactus in the corner. That was a fun night."

"It was. But focus, please. Yes, that's Blaze. I invited him over tonight." Pausing, I puff out a breath. "I offered to teach him how to whittle. In my shop."

Her gum pops and I wait for her to tell me I'm off my rocker or something. I've taught many people to whittle over the years, but I've never invited them over for it. Or showed them my shop. Few people have seen the inside of my shop.

"So you're letting him in the workshop for the first time with his fine ass? Sounds serious."

"I just kind of blurted it out to teach him and he was so excited to know I had a garage workshop. I didn't want to tell him I have a thing about people being in there."

A flash of headlights bounces off the windows and the crunch of tires announces Blaze is already here.

"He just pulled up. I'll have to talk to you later. Love you."

"You'll be fine! Go get em'" She roars like a tiger as I end the call. Not the conversation I needed, but it will have to do.

Exiting the house, I step out before Blaze can knock.

"Hi!"

His breath hangs in the crisp night air and I shiver, not prepared for the goosebumps racing up my flesh under my sweater.

"Hey, that didn't take you long to get here."

Blaze smiles again, and it's a special kind of smile. Like it's only for me.

"Well, I don't waste any time when I have someone waiting for me."

I don't know how to respond to that, so I motion for him to take the short path to my shop.

We walk side by side, and when we reach the door, I pause.

Swallowing, I turn to him. This shouldn't be a big deal, really, but it is.

"Welcome to my workshop."

CHAPTER 8

BLAZE

River bites his lip as he holds the door of his shop open for me.

"Is something wrong?"

I take a step back from the door to make it easier if he's changed his mind. The whole way up the short path, I felt his wound up energy and didn't miss how he kept shoving his hands in and out of his pockets. His usual level of Zen was nowhere close.

"No, it's fine. When you're inside... well, you'll see. Come on."

River enters and flicks on the light for us and after a moment, the fluorescent lights stop stuttering and shine their full brightness.

"Holy shit, River. This is... it's... wow."

The place is immaculate. Stacks of lumber are so neatly organized, I'd consider teasing him over his attention to detail if I didn't think he was proud of it. He'd stacked the lumber to help Heath just like this so it must make his work easier. There are tools I don't even know what they do, all in their own little places. Some are hanging and some on shelves. There's not a speck of sawdust or wood shaving to be found, but it carries that scent of newly cut wood.

But that's not the part that has my jaw hanging to the floor.

It's the sheer number of projects in various stages of finishing. All of them are beautiful even when partially done.

"I don't think I've ever made anyone speechless before."

River is waiting for me to say something, and I don't know if I can.

"When do you make all this? How?" I cross the room to a dining room table he's not quite finished, trailing my fingers over the intricate carving on the backs of the dining room chairs. God, his talent is incredible.

"Like I said earlier. I come here when I can't sleep and I work on something."

I point to the carved sign hanging above what must be his main work area. "You make that?"

He nods and his cheeks turn pink. "One of my very first projects. It's not very good. I've come a long way since then."

Raising an eyebrow, I lean in closer. It might not have the detail of the tiny candies he carved for Colby's shop, but it's still amazing. Especially if it was one of his first projects. He most definitely had raw talent.

"I won't agree with you because I think it's fantastic. How come you don't do this full time?" I run my hand over a doll cradle he has on the go with a smile. My business mind goes crazy with ideas. This kind of quality stuff sells high in the right market. He could do what he loves all the time if he wanted to.

Turning to voice this, he's already shaking his head. "I know what you're thinking and I can't. I don't have the time or the stock to make a predictable income. That's why it's a side business. Even if I had the time, I'm not sure it would generate enough to support me." He laughs. "I should have known you'd recognize the opportunity right away. You're not the first one to suggest it."

"Who was the first?"

And why does it matter to me that someone else had the idea before I did?

"Nobody I know personally. It's just what everyone says whenever I make it to a craft market or other kind of thing." He shrugs, like it's no big deal, as he pulls out a few small pieces of wood and tools. "Trust me. I'd be making all kinds of things if I had more time." He aims his smile my way. "But I don't and that's why I do what I can."

"As long as you're happy. That's what matters most."

I think he's happy. He's never not laid back and smiling. River has the patience of a saint, and I don't think he's ever voiced displeasure over a damn thing. Even when I stabbed him with a vaccine. Which, oddly enough, was a pleasure for me to have him sit and let me take care of it.

"I thought I'd teach you how to carve a spoon. It's super easy and I can show you the basic strokes all with one tool."

I snort like a grade school boy. "Stroking the tool. Got it."

River cocks his head with a tiny smile. "So it's gonna be like that, is it?"

"I'm total grade school humour, River. How do you not know this?"

He bustles about and pulls two chairs for us to sit on.

"I guess because you always take charge at the ranch. And when I sort of tried to joke with you, it was like you froze up. I thought maybe I crossed the line. But you're more serious than playful."

He's not wrong. I used to be playful before I always had to behave like a respectable CEO. I got so used to checking my language and behaviour it became second nature. My ex frowned upon any actions that didn't fit the corporate image of Blaze Porter, CEO. Too many years passed before I realized there was no difference between Blaze Porter CEO and Blaze Porter, the regular guy. I had become someone I wasn't and I've missed this part of me. Maybe more than I thought.

Clearing my throat, I find his gaze on me and those brown eyes encourage me to say more. "It's, ah, somethin' I'm allowin' myself to do more of now that I've left the old life behind. I'm more comfortable here. I didn't think I'd not shown you this side much."

"Oh, you have. Just in little bits here and there when you think nobody is watching." River licks his lips and locks eyes with me. "It's just nice to see you so... open."

Even though he seemed weirded out to let me in here, I'm relaxed. But that could be because of the man I'm next to and not the space itself.

River hands me a square block of wood and I chortle again.

"Now what?"

"You gave me wood." This time I snort laugh. It's not even that funny, but fuck, the way River laughs along with me? I can make stupid jokes all night if he wants.

River, with a mischievous twinkle in his eye, leans closer. "Did I?"

For a minute I forget what he's even talking about because his warm breath so close to me has my brain freeze up.

"Did you what?"

"Give you wood?"

River licks his lips and turns away, leaving me wondering if we're flirting now or is this just the two of us being goofy?

"Whittling is a lot of fun once you learn the techniques. It can morph into intricate carving pretty quick once you find a love for it. Honestly, a spoon will be really easy once you master the strokes."

I can't help it and bark more laughter. What is it about him and being here that has me dropping my guard so easily? Maybe it's because of nerves with him being so... how come I never noticed the silver flecks in his hair before?

"Right. Master stroker. Got it." I snicker.

He tilts his head again, his lips twitch and I'm pretty sure he wants to make a joke too, but he holds up a knife.

"This is a simple jackknife." He hands me the knife, blade open and handle pointed to me. "It's the easiest thing to carry in your pocket so you can carve on most anything. I'll show you the main strokes."

This time I know he's joking, since he quietly snorts with a shake of his head.

"Right. Strokes and wood. I'll try not to make it sexual." I say, but my body is shaking with laughter. When has it been this fun to be so immature? To not care about expectations or etiquette and just be myself?

Sure, I've been more myself since I'd got back to the ranch, but this is different. The expectation to behave a certain way isn't sitting on my shoulders. River likes it and encourages it. I like to see him smile. Since the first day we worked together, his smile was something I'd looked forward to.

He opens his knife. "The biggest rule you need to remember is never carve the blade towards you. It's always away from your belly and into your buddy."

"So it's better to make my friend bleed? That seems cruel."

"Okay, an imaginary buddy then." He shows me how to hold the knife. "This is a simple straightaway cut. You'll use this the most, especially when you're making something small out of something so big."

Holding the block of wood like he is, I copy his movements and for several minutes, all I'm doing is removing a lot of wood at once and getting a feel of the knife in my hand. It's sharp, and it's like slicing a warm knife through butter. He tells me to keep my wrist locked to stay straight. The repetitive motion is actually very calming and while my hand aches a little from gripping the knife, it's a very peaceful activity.

"You're doing great, Blaze. Do you want to learn another stroke?"

"I like this. Do you think I'll actually make a spoon?"

He smiles at me and... wow. It kinda takes my breath away. His short brown hair needs a trim, it curls around his ears, but it suits him. His eyes smile along with his lips and thank god he speaks because I forgot the conversation.

"You will make several spoons under my watch. I guarantee it."

River shows me how to do a short, controlled stroke called a thumb push. It's how I can make shorter strokes for detail while still pointing the blade away from me.

"There's another short stroke that's pointing the blade towards you, but I don't think you're ready for that yet. We'll cover that another night." He pauses. "Assuming you'll still want to see me again." He rushes to add. "To learn I mean."

We have one of those weird moments again, and it's like River sees right through me. Like I'm naked in front of him and... shit, I need to shut that train of thought down or I'll have two chunks of wood to deal with.

Clearing my throat, I wiggle my block. "Why wouldn't I? This is great. Look at how my block is now a... smaller block!"

River nods, looking away before meeting my gaze again.

"Would you ever consider going out with me?"

My soon to be spoon thumps to the floor and he rushes to pick it up. "Sorry, forget I asked."

He hands me back the wood I dropped with his gaze on the floor.

"No, I can't forget you said that."

Because I think I hoped one of us would say it and I'm not brave enough yet to go first.

"Sorry, I made it weird. Let's just move on."

He busies himself carving his piece of wood, and the silence around us crackles with nerves. If I stay quiet, I might lose this chance forever.

"I'd more than consider it. I'd say yes." I croak.

He pauses his carving, keeping his eyes on his project. "You'd go out with me? On a real date?"

"Yes, a real date."

As a smile returns to his adorable face, the tension in my gut loosens

"Okay. Good. Um...," He laughs and runs a hand through his hair. "I didn't think I'd ask you out tonight. This has been... enlightening."

I grab a broom from the corner and sweep up the mess we made, but it's mostly to distract myself from the enormity of the step I just took.

"If it makes you feel better, I haven't been this relaxed or at peace with myself since I left my company. Datin' should be somethin' that's on my mind. It's been far too long since I've ah...," I clear my throat, suddenly awkward at the thought of sex with River in my mind.

"Heh, yeah, you don't have to say it. I don't date much. It's just one of those things, you know? You get lost in your life and then before you know it, boom, you're single and forty."

I dump the swept up shavings in the can by his counter and lean against it.

"I had a lot of fun tonight, River. Laughin' is somethin' I've been without for too long. There are reasons but... I like you."

He smiles that panty melting smile again and... oof. How did I keep him at arm's length this whole time? Because there's a lot to River to like and we've only just started.

"I like you too, but we need to be up early. Can we discuss the next step tomorrow?"

With a grin, I shake my head. "This sounds like a business deal."

He laughs again and when he oozes that sexy smile, my brain checks out. I have been willfully blind and isn't that a reality check to see what's in front of me finally?

"Okay, how about this? We won't talk tomorrow and instead I'll show up at your place at 6 P.M. Is that better?"

"When was datin' so fuckin' awkward?" I laugh as I shrug my jacket on.

"It's only awkward when two guys out of practice try to give it a whirl."

He opens the shop door and walks me to my truck. I slide behind the wheel, but before I close the door, I have one last thing.

"I look forward to the practice then, River. See you tomorrow."

I back out of the driveway, leaving him smiling like a fool.

Pretty sure the same smile is on my face, too.

CHAPTER 9

RIVER

"**I**s this where I put the nails, River?"

Heath, thank god, is waiting before operating the nail gun because he's about to drive a nail through not only the wood but likely his hand.

"Lay it to the side please, Heath, finger off the trigger." Thankfully, he does as I ask right away. "Let's take ten, okay?"

"Sure! I'm gonna go see the llamas if Dante is there and I'll be back."

Heath trots off to the llama barn and I call after him. "Ten minutes only Heath! We want to finish today!"

Turning, he gives me a thumbs up and trips but doesn't fall. Small miracle.

I didn't sleep a wink last night. On a constant replay is my time with Blaze. The way he opened up a new side to him with his juvenile sense of humour was unexpected. I loved how we could laugh like kids, and it didn't matter to anyone. But the memory that lingers strongest is the soft lilt to his voice when he said he'd go out with me. I still can't believe he said yes.

I asked Blaze out, and he said yes. My sinfully hot work partner at the ranch is going on a date with me. And my obsession with it distracted me enough I almost let Heath nail his hand to a board. So much for me being the responsible one here.

"Is everythin' okay?" Blaze comes over from where he's been drilling holes for the fence posts. He shouldn't be looking so sexy after all the heavy labour but holy crap, I'd climb him like a tree right now if I could. His forehead shines with sweat and he's rolled up his sleeves, drawing my attention to his muscular arms. Forearm porn is real and he could be a model for it.

"It's great. Just sent Heath on a break. We're learning the nail gun, and I need to make sure he doesn't hurt himself."

The colour drops from Blaze's face. "Oh god, please don't need a hospital visit today. I'm not good with too much gore."

"What are you talking about? You deliver horses and clean gross wounds and all kinds of stuff. How can a nail gun injury bother you?"

He cocks his head with a little scratch to his scruff. "Probably because it's a human. Like when I vaccinated you by accident? I threw up later. It freaked me out."

"You did? I suppose that makes sense. I'll make sure Heath stays safe. How are the fence holes going?"

Blaze twists behind him with a hand through his hair and I glue my gaze to his bicep as it flexes. Such an innocent motion and movement. I'm dialed into it, though. Since he agreed to go out with me and we flirted last night, I feel like it's okay to appreciate him out in the open now. For months I've been hiding it because I wasn't sure about him. I'm still not. But I'm closer to finding out what he's like, at least.

"River?"

"Huh?"

"While I appreciate the oglin', you didn't hear a word I said."

Oh fuck. I zoned out that much? Maybe I shouldn't let Heath use the nail gun today at all if I'm going to be like this.

Clearing my throat, I meet his eyes and I'm relieved to see them shine with a boyish delight. The little smirk on his lips will be the death of me.

"Sorry, what were you saying?"

He opens his mouth, but tilts his chin to look behind me. Heath is returning on time and it's time for me to focus and keep us all injury free.

"Okay, River. I'm back! Can we nail stuff now?"

Blaze laughs low, and the sound feeds the fire in my belly. Only I can hear him say, "Yeah, River, can we nail somethin' now?"

Swallowing hard, I can only stare at him as he laughs silently and winks at me. "Just keep the kid in one piece and no gore. I have faith in you."

Heath arrives all innocent and happy, jabbering away about llamas and how soft they are and Dante making soap or some shit. He reminds me of a golden retriever. Constantly happy and moving. Blaze moves back to his post holes, and it's with great effort I focus on Heath.

Enormous really. I deserve a medal.

"Change of plans, buddy. We're gonna use the hammer instead. Not every job site will have power tools. In fact, some companies you might work for won't supply them at all. So if you wanted an air nailer you'd have to bring it yourself. The hammer will always work and never let you down."

"That makes sense. How do you know all this?"

Moving the nail gun out of the way, I hand him a hammer and set a package of nails next to where he's kneeling.

"I worked for a few construction companies when I was younger." I settle next to him and show him how to hammer and hold the nail. It seems easy, but it takes a bit of practice to get it right and not slam your thumb.

Heath tries it and doesn't do too bad. The nail went straight and there's no smashed thumb. That's a win. I watch him do a few more and I move over to my section.

"You're getting the hang of it. It's harder than it looks."

Heath nods, not taking his eyes off the job and a swell of pride rushes out of nowhere for his progress. He'll find his calling one day. Maybe it might be carpentry.

"So how come you left construction?"

"Oh, I never really left. I have my side business. I just don't work for contractors anymore. It was mostly summer jobs as a teenager. Then it was just jobs here and there as companies needed it."

He pauses for more nails and moves to the next section. "So you prefer ranch work then? Why choose this over building since you love it so much?"

Leave it to Heath to ask a harmless question that's anything but to me. "It's not that I prefer it, it's more that I needed it." Heath seems to pick up on my discomfort with the question and moves on.

It was a wise choice to go with the hammer. Heath is moving along faster than I am and all the pieces for the coop are almost done. We're on time to put it all together tomorrow and finish with the fence. My gaze drifts to Blaze again, and I watch him manhandling the posts into holes.

And that's when it happens.

"Ow, fuck, fuck, fuck!"

Dropping my hammer, I rip off my glove and watch my thumb rapidly swell and turn an alarming shade of purple.

"River! Are you okay?" Heath helps me up off the ground and leads me to the first aid kit. "What do I do?"

"Go to the house and ask Dan for an ice pack and towel."

He nods and scampers off, leaving me puffing through the pain as I silently berate myself for not paying attention. Thank god it wasn't Heath that was hurt.

"River, are you okay? What happened?"

Blaze gently takes my hand and winces at my mashed thumb.

"If you wanted to get out of our date, you didn't have to maim yourself. A guy might take it personally you've gone to such levels."

He's kidding and his eyes are warm with concern as he gently caresses my arm. I don't even think he's aware he's doing it.

"The only thing you should take personally is I smashed my thumb while I was watching you."

Another one of those awkward silences passes and it's only interrupted with Heath returning with the ice and towel.

Blaze takes it from him and, with a gentle touch, he holds the wrapped ice pack against my throbbing thumb.

"I bet you thought it would be me smashing my thumb, eh, Blaze?"

Heath jokes and I'm grateful for it because Blaze was on the verge of saying something.

"I sure did. Can you keep up what you were doin' without us for a few minutes?"

"We're almost done with the ramp, River said. Once that's finished, I think we're waiting for tomorrow to put it all together."

"Right. If you can finish those last pieces, I'm going to sit on the porch for a few with Blaze and I'll come back."

"You got it!"

Heath dutifully returns to his job, and Blaze's blue eyes lock on mine.

"You sure you're okay?"

"Once the sting and the nausea passes, I'll be okay. Sit with me?"

Nodding, he walks along with me, his hand on my back, to the porch. We sit on the porch swing and I lean forward, dropping my head to my knees. I did a good job. My thumb throbs to the beat of my heart and while I'm not in danger of passing out, I need to get my wits about me.

Blaze strokes my back in silence and when I finally sit up again, I don't think he's even aware of his comforting gestures. But I sure am.

The hollow sounds of Heath hammering nails in the distance is a good sign he's managing on his own.

"So," Blaze begins. "Do you need me to drive you home?"

"I'll be okay. The ice is helping. It's going to be a bitch to use for a few days, but I'll survive."

Blaze nods and he still hasn't taken his hand off my back, even though I sat up.

"At the risk of sounding like I don't care about your well bein', are we still on tonight? I'll be disappointed, but if you want to just chill out and rest, I understand."

He'll be disappointed? Be still my heart.

"Actually, to chill and rest sounds good." Fuck, his smile fades and I rush to add, "But if you don't mind, I'd like to do it with you."

Blaze twists his head my way. "You askin' me to Netflix and chill tonight, River?" His smile returns full force. "If so, that's a hell yes."

Again with the loopy smiles and silence. What exactly is happening here?

"Hey, uh, guys?" Heath calls and we both stand. "I think I'm done."

We both walk back to where Heath has finished our project without injury.

"You are done! Excellent work Heath!" I pat him on the back with my good hand. "Let's call it a day. Gather all the tools and tomorrow we'll finish this up, so Dan has a home for his chickens."

After we've cleaned up and Heath still hasn't hurt himself, I chalk it up to me being the injury of the day. Blaze rests against his truck, clearly waiting for me, and my pulse picks up another notch.

"You sure you're okay to drive?"

"I'll be okay. It's a swollen thumb." I fumble my keys with my injured hand and Blaze raises an eyebrow.

"You sure?"

"Yes, I'm sure. So, ah... your place or mine for tonight?" I grin like a fool since we can't seem to stop these ridiculous lines and jokes. "I don't mean to sound like a sleazy guy at a bar, but it is the question."

"I'll come to yours and bring you dinner. Just ice that and take something for pain. See you around six again, if that's okay?"

"Yeah, it's perfect."

Too fucking perfect.

Now if only my dick would stop throbbing like my thumb.

Chapter 10

Blaze

id River really ask me to Netflix and chill?

Or am I out of touch and that means exactly what it means? Dear lord, shoot me now. I don't know how to proceed and now I'm sweating like I'm walking in the desert over a common phrase that I may or may not have misunderstood.

Heather will know what to do. Freshly showered, I put her on speakerphone and pace my room wondering what the hell I should wear.

"Hey Blaze! How are things?"

"I need your help."

"What's wrong? You sound like you might throw up? Did you eat bad left overs again?"

"What? No. Listen, I ah... remember the guy I told you about? I vaccinated him by accident a while ago?"

"Oh! The tall drink of River? That one?"

Did I actually say that?

"Yeah, River. So we've had a change in the friendship and I'm going to his place tonight."

"For what? A date?"

I pause at my closet debating on the Henley or a button down. I choose the Henley since it's my favourite colour.

"Um, yeah. It's Netflix and chill? Well, it's really to chill because he hurt himself today and we were supposed to go out, but then I got bossy and said, no you should chill. And then he said I'd love to but with you. Not to mention we've been slidin' in all these flirty innuendos for two days, and he's teachin' me to carve a spoon, Heather. A spoon. I'm doin' somethin' with my hands again other than spreadsheets and emails. He's so fuckin' sweet and funny. I'm nervous and I don't know what to wear."

I suck in a breath after that spew of words and other than the shirt, I'm still not dressed and staring at the phone on my bed, waiting for Heather to say something.

"That's a lot to unpack, Blaze. Are you letting what Ted did make you doubt his interest? Because you shouldn't."

Ted is my ex. We dated for two years and I thought he was in love with me. I sure loved him. But it took an overheard phone conversation to find out he didn't feel that way about me at all. He stole a lot of my confidence along with some of my bank balance when I told him to fuck off after that.

"Well, I think most of Ted has washed off. We were makin' all kinds of jokes about wood and strokin' and it was a lot of fun. River even mentioned he hadn't seen me like that and it was nice."

"Just be yourself then. He obviously likes the real you. What are you wearing? Is this actually a chilled evening or are you hoping to chill under the sheets?"

"Uh, I don't know? I think actual chill since he hurt himself. Honestly, I don't know. You know I've been checkin' him out since I got here, and I didn't think a guy like him would be interested. Now he is and I guess I'm.... out of practice?"

Jesus, I'm babbling on like a damn fool. Was I always like this over guys I liked?

"Okay, sweetie. Take a breath. It's a date, not an execution. These things are supposed to be fun and I'm willing to bet it won't matter what you wear because it will be on the floor. So let's move on to the sex talk."

"Oh god, Heather. Am I ready for that?"

Flopping on the bed next to the phone, I throw my arm over my eyes. Heather and I have talked about a lot of things and she has young teenage kids. She's had the sex talk with them and as much as we are close in age and she's my best friend, she's about to go all mom on me. But I appreciate it because I honestly don't know if I'm ready.

"Blaze, you've been single and haven't even had a one nighter in over two years. If now isn't the time, I don't know what else you're waiting for. You said he's cute and funny and you've been watching him since you got there. From what you've told me, you're quite smitten, even if you don't want to admit it."

Groaning, I know she's right.

"Just like ridin' a bike, right?"

"Something like that. Just be safe. You're adults, so talk about it and you'll know if it's right. He's not Ted. So stop thinking like that. If River is into you, see where it goes. You deserve to be happy, my love."

"I know, I just... I don't want my heart crushed again, Heather."

"Blaze, if I could guarantee that won't happen, I would. Wear the red Henley, bring some condoms and have fun for one night. You're allowed."

"I picked that shirt, actually. Thanks for this. You know me better than Dan some days. I'll be safe... mom."

I laugh and Heather joins in.

"Go on then and text me tomorrow. Be safe!"

Laughing, I end the call, no less nervous than I was before, but one thing Heather is right about is River isn't Ted. He stripped me, a confident billionaire businessman, of my self worth and confidence and I still hate him for it. It's taken me so long to even feel remotely close to what I used to be.

But I've never wilted away from my life. With head held high, I moved on. I pushed my company to the top, and I ate ice cream at home in private with tears in my eyes occasionally, but I never gave up.

And I want River. I do. But there's so much we still need to know about each other and... I'm more than a little scared. I'm terrified of putting myself out there only to be crushed again.

My phone chirps with a text and I think it might be Heather giving me a final thumbs up, but it's River.

My heart damn near jumps through my ribs as I read his text.

River: Hey, I made dinner, if you don't mind. If you like pasta primavera, I'll have it ready for when you get here.

Blaze: I love primavera! You sure you didn't hurt yourself cooking? I was bringing dinner so you could rest.

River: Thank you, but I'm okay. Just get your fine ass over here.

Blaze: Wow. On my way.

Rushing around the room, I pull on a pair of black khaki dress pants. It's a date so I should wear something other than jeans. I'll also make the extra effort and spritz some cologne on that I no longer wear. The citrusy scent rushes me back to my old life and, oddly, reminds me of who I was. No, who I still am.

I'm Blaze fucking Porter and I never back down.

With that rush of confidence, I grab a condom from my night-stand and shove it in my pocket. After a moment of deliberation, I go back and grab a second one. Not because I'm confident we'll have sex twice. I'm not eighteen anymore. It's more of an insurance in case I get that far and fuck it up the first time.

Clutching the bottle of Sauvignon Blanc, I walk to River's door and already the aroma of garlic greets me. With a glance around, I notice the fume hood from his stove nearby and smile. He's actually cooking and I can't recall when I've ever had a date with a home cooked meal.

My dates were always high-end restaurants and fancy theatres. Stuff that cost a lot of money and never allowed you to really connect with or know someone. Isn't that a revelation to have as I'm standing on River's doorstep? Not once did Ted ever cook for me or me for him. We were always out at some function or restaurant surrounded by crowds of people. The only time we were ever truly alone was in bed.

"Hey! I didn't hear you knock. Come on in."

River has opened the door while I stand there, wine bottle in one hand and the other one in my pocket. He catches me off guard. Not just for opening the door while I'm having a moment, but he's also changed clothes. And he looks amazing.

His short shaggy brown hair is still wet from a shower. He's rolled up the sleeves of a white button-down shirt and he also went with a pair of khaki pants. His are navy blue and he's barefoot. I don't know why him being barefoot for our date sends goosebumps racing up my skin, but I know I like it.

"Hi. You look great." I gulp and raise the bottle in my hand. "I brought wine."

River smiles at me and my knees wobble as he motions for me to come in.

"Thank you. You clean up pretty good yourself." My cheeks heat and he winks. "I hope you don't mind I cooked. I didn't want all the produce to go to waste. I know you said you'd bring something over. You're not mad, are you?"

The whole time he talks he's walked into the kitchen and set the wine on a table. A table he's already set and there are fresh flowers in an old mason jar with little tea light candles.

Oh boy.

This is the date of all dates in my books, and we've not even started.

"Blaze?"

When River notices I didn't follow him, he turns around to find me glued in place still in his front entrance.

"Is everything okay?"

His hand on my arm as his warm brown eyes look up at me almost do me in.

"I'm great. No, I'm not mad at all. This is... nice. You're supposed to be restin' and you did all this."

Finally kicking off my shoes, I move into the kitchen with him. He drains pasta and finishes cooking vegetables before adding them to a white sauce.

"It's not that bad. I took a pain reliever earlier and I might lose the nail, but I'm doing okay. We'll rest later."

"Can I help you with anythin'?"

"Sure. There are wine glasses in the cupboard in the corner. Should be a corkscrew there, too. Why don't you pour our glasses while I plate the food?"

Nodding, I find the glasses and corkscrew and pour us each a glass of wine as he sets two plates of food down at the table.

"Where did you get the flowers?" I ask as he pulls out a chair for me. With a smile, I seat myself as he takes the chair across from me.

"I stopped at the corner store on my way home. There's a family that cuts sunflowers and gladiolas to sell. They have a greenhouse and have most kinds of flowers. I hoped they had been by today to refill the display. Do you like sunflowers?"

"I do. I like most flowers, actually."

"Any favourites?" River spreads a napkin over his lap while I do the same.

"I've always loved tulips and daffodils. Spring flowers. They're the first hope after a long winter and their colours always make me smile. Did you know daffodils represent new beginnin'?"

"No, I didn't. But that makes sense with them being spring flowers. What about tulips? Do they mean anything?"

"Um... yeah... they represent different feelin's dependin' on their colours. They're a romantic flower. More than roses. Even sunflowers have meanin'."

I must sound like such a fool going on about flowers, but River is listening like it's the most riveting of topics. For some reason, that attention makes me keep on spewing more flower trivia like a five-year-old with too many facts in their brain.

"Yellow sunflowers are often for happiness, but they can also symbolize loyalty and adoration. Like tulips, all the colours mean somethin' different. I mean, if you want them to. They could also just be, hey I like you here are some flowers."

River smiles, soft and warm, and I rub at my chest. I've never told anyone all that before.

"I'll have to remember that then. I didn't know colours of flowers meant different things." He takes a bite of his dinner and, after swallowing, he notices I haven't touched my food yet.

"Are you going to eat with me? Or is this a spectator event?"

I laugh softly. "I'll eat. I just wasn't expecting you to have cooked or set a table with flowers and candles. It's very... intimate."

River takes a sip of his wine before assessing me with his kind eyes.

"It's a date and you're my guest. My mom always said when you have someone special over, you treat them special."

I don't know how to respond to that, being called special. Until I can trust myself to speak, I nod and take a mouthful of the pasta instead.

"Ohmygod River, this is amazin'. You made this all from scratch?"

His smile is reward enough as he continues to eat and tells me how he made the sauce from a low fat recipe his mom used to make.

"I had planned to make it a few days ago. When I stopped at the grocery store, some guy hit on me in the produce section too."

"People do that? What did he say?"

"He asked me if I prefer eggplant or zucchini. It was really quite vulgar and honestly, bizarre. Like who thinks flirting with a zucchini is attractive?"

"Indeed." I snort laugh, trying to picture it in my brain. "Was he cute at least? Did he give you a number? How would that even work?"

River laughs more. "No number. But he mentioned he does his shopping every Wednesday afternoon if I changed my mind."

"Well, it's good to keep your options open."

"Nah, I don't want options."

His eyes burn into me, and I shift on my chair.

Okay. We're past innocent flirting. I'm not that much out of the game to know that comment was for me. But, I need more time to settle and I quickly change the topic.

We chat some more about farmers' markets, local flower sellers, his cooking, and me working on my carving after we finish the chicken coop. But the entire time we've talked, there's a building hum of anticipation. I want to ask him a million questions and know who he is inside and out. But my libido is roaring back to life with every lick of his lips and soft laugh.

I want all the romance and intimate dinners at home like this. I want to hear about his family and his life, and I want to kiss him.

If I don't get to kiss him soon, I might die.

Cleaning the table together, he stacks the dishes next to the sink before dealing with the leftovers.

"Okay, we can go sit —"

Stepping into his small space, I drop my hands on either side of his head and trap him against the refrigerator.

"I'm sorry to cut you off, but River, you have to know I'm attracted to you. If I have to watch your tongue touch your lips anymore without me kissin' you, I might actually do somethin' stupid." His eyes widen as I dip my head closer to his ear. "Please, can I kiss you?"

"Depends on what the something stupid is?" He whispers, but he's turned his face closer to mine and his hand rests on my chest.

"I don't know yet, but I'm pretty creative. I'm sure it would be memorable."

He laughs and his hand curls into my shirt. "I bet the first time you kiss me while pressed against my fridge will be memorable, too."

Easing back, I drink in the gorgeous man in front of me as he licks his lips and pulls me closer. "You can kiss me, Blaze. I've wanted you to since I first met you."

So many thoughts run through my mind as I bring my mouth to his. Soft or hard. How much tongue? He seems sweet, but maybe he wants a passionate kiss. I overthink all the things that matter to me and this matters to me more than selling my business right now.

When my lips press against his, he immediately opens and darts his tongue out. I welcome it with greed and press harder into his mouth. Both of River's hands clutch my shirt as he returns the kiss and pulls me closer. My hips roll into his, wallpapering us against the common kitchen appliance like an obscene fridge magnet.

When we finally break the kiss, I cradle his face in my hands before kissing him again, softer this time and with genuine affection. I linger there, my lips with his, committing the plush softness of them to memory. He shivers against me and I take a moment to commit every single thing about this kiss to my memory. From the lingering taste of the wine on his tongue, to the way he softly sighed and clutched me to him, this will be a memory to warm me on the coldest of days. I step back with a swallow.

"Was that memorable enough for you?"

I'm pleased to see River's eyes glazed. Although that could be from the painkiller.

"I'd hate to see when you do something stupid if that's what you do for memorable." He runs his fingers through my short beard.

"I've always wondered if your beard was as soft as it is shiny."

"And is it?"

"Feels like rabbit fur."

"Do not tell the guys I'm soft like a bunny. I have a reputation to uphold." Taking his hand, I lead him over to the sofa.

"Shall we move to the Netflix part of the evening?"

Chapter 11

River

Holy-Oh-Fuck.

Blaze can kiss.

It's been a long time since anyone has laid their lips against mine. Even longer since a kiss has left me dazed and breathless. If I give myself a minute to think, I don't think I've ever felt this tingling, this entire body awareness from a kiss. I wanted to crawl into his lap and never let him go.

Midnight walks to the fridge will never be the same now.

This is not how I pictured the night to play out. I thought we would talk and get to know each other. Have some laughs over dinner. Maybe a kiss goodbye at the door and plans for another date.

But then we had wine and more than just laughs. I had to make sure he knew I was a thousand percent into him because he still has this shell up. A thick shell he must have reasons for having, but I cracked it the other night, and a little more today. I want the whole of what's inside, because the parts I've seen so far I like very much. If the kiss we just shared is anything to go by, he's willing to let me in.

Blaze settles himself on my sofa with a sigh.

"This is so comfortable. It feels like a cloud. You must fall asleep here a lot."

Sitting next to him, I rest my head back into the puffy couch. "I've fallen asleep here more times than I can count. I won't lie. My bedroom is six feet away, but it always seems so far once I sit here."

Blaze shifts and I crack an eye open to see what he's doing. He's turned himself to face me and tucked one of his feet up under him. I don't know why, but the position has me turn my head towards him with a smile.

"Do you really want to watch Netflix?"

He shrugs and a tilt to his lips makes my breath catch in my throat. "Heather told me that phrase doesn't translate literally. Which I sort of knew already, but I'm also not opposed to watchin' somethin'." He reaches a hand over, dusting his fingertips across my jaw. "I kind of want to talk, though."

Shivering at his gentle touch, I sit up and mirror his position, tucking a foot under my thigh.

"What do you want to talk about first?"

Blaze hesitates before meeting my gaze. "When you had me in your workshop, you seemed uncomfortable to have me in there. Did I imagine that?"

Puffing my cheeks, I huff a small laugh. "Going for the big question right away. You didn't imagine it, but I was okay with you there."

It should be odd or maybe even scary to tell someone other than Kelly about my sometime hang up with having people there. But I like Blaze and I'm comfortable with him. We could build something beautiful if we're open and honest from the very beginning. I feel that to the edge of my soul. I'm too old for games and secrets.

I'd rather find out now if we're only compatible with matters of the body and not the mind.

"I think I mentioned before that I spent a lot of time with my mom when she was sick. I was still a young teenager. But mom and I were close. She was my rock. My parents had me late in life because my mom was told she'd never be able to have kids. They kind of stopped thinking about it and then boom, happy accident."

Blaze laughs but reaches for my hand, and I allow him to thread his fingers through mine.

"You were the best accident, I'm sure. Your mom was proud of you. That I don't even question."

"She was. I know it. Her and dad were forty-five and new parents. I totally changed their life, and I was very lucky to have such amazing parents." I swallow hard as the familiar tears prick behind my eyes. "Anyway, we were a close knit family and when my mom got sick, I couldn't stand knowing she was home alone. My dad still worked because there were bills to pay, right? We had a home care nurse come by twice a week when she got worse, but I didn't want her to be alone. I was a momma's boy."

I smile sadly, and Blaze surprises me with a kiss to my hand. "You were a good son. Still are. There's nothin' to be ashamed of for lovin' your mom."

"Thank you. Anyway, when mom finally passed away, it was with me and Dad, so it was worth it to be there. Back to your question about the shop. My mom had a life insurance policy, and it was all for me. It wasn't a lot, but it was exactly what I needed. Her policy bought me that space and the tools. She knew I liked to build and carve. I carved by her bedside all the time and showed her what I made. She saw my talent long before I did. Dad helped me with it all and I don't like other people in there sometimes because it makes me feel... "

I don't really know how to explain it. But Blaze does.

"Like your safe place isn't safe anymore? Too many people in there make you feel vulnerable all over again?"

"Yeah. That's... accurate."

I notice how he looks down at our joined hands and not at me.

"What happened to you? I was struggling to find words to tell you that, but you get it right away."

"Do we really want to get into my emotional scars tonight, too? You're already exhausted from dinner and sharin' that with me. You're supposed to be restin'. How's the thumb, anyway?"

Raising my other hand, I show him. Blaze wrinkles his nose, making me laugh.

"Jeeze, Riv. That's gotta hurt. How are we goin' to finish buildin' that chicken coop with your thumb like this?"

"Oh, I'll be the supervisor and tell you what to do." I wink and Blaze laughs a full, deep laugh. He's gorgeous when he laughs like that. The little crinkles around his eyes are deeper and... fuck, even the sound of his laugh does something to my insides.

His eyes darken as he leans forward. "You want to boss me around, River? What do you want me to do right now?"

Is this real life right now or am I loopy on a glass of wine and an ibuprofen?

He's leaned so close to me I lick my lips, anticipating a kiss, but he waits.

"I want you to kiss me again." My voice sounds foreign. Thick, low and oozing with so much desire, I'm almost embarrassed.

Almost.

But Blaze moves the extra distance with his lips hovering over mine. "I can do that."

With a tenderness he didn't have earlier when he devoured me against the fridge, his lips brush mine. Over and over, his kisses taste and tease. He runs his tongue over my bottom lip and his fingers find their way behind my head, pulling me closer to him. His gentle yet passionate handling of me turns me into a puddle of sighing goo.

It's almost too much, too intimate. When he eases back to rest his forehead against mine, I'm left panting and clawing at his chest to anchor myself in reality.

"River..." Blaze breathes and never has my name ever sounded so revered. "Fuck... I could do this all night. You're sumthin' else."

"What's stopping you?" Sliding my hand up his chest, I curl my fingers around his neck as he shifts away from me.

"Promise not to laugh?"

A laugh squeaks out, and he raises an eyebrow.

"That one doesn't count! I promise I won't laugh."

Blaze sighs and drops his gaze. "I'm a little old-fashioned. I've been... burned before. Full disclosure, though, I brought two condoms with me tonight because I didn't know how anythin' would go." He lifts his head with a shy smile that lands right in my heart. "Heather gave me the safe sex talk, and I panicked. But River, fuck, this is gonna sound so dumb."

"It's not dumb. I'm listening and I won't laugh. Promise."

He sighs again before meeting my gaze. "I want us to date. Flowers at the door, sexy texts, road trips, whatever couples do now to get to know each other. I don't want to skip that. While I admit I want sex, I also want to know you. I think that means we shouldn't have sex on the first date. I want to, badly, but... I think I should wait with you."

Well, I wasn't expecting that. Not even close.

"I'm all in if you are. There's something about you, Blaze, that I'm more than willing to be patient and wait for."

"Really?"

Wiggling closer to him, I place a tender kiss on his lips. "I've been watching you for months, wondering if your beard felt as soft as it looked. Wondering what you'd look like in the morning laying in bed and if you were a snuggler. And what made a billionaire come to a rescue ranch and walk away from his life?" I drop another kiss. "I want to know you, too. And I can wait."

"It won't be easy, though." I add as I sit back to resist the temptation of more.

"No, it won't be, but... " He hides a yawn behind his hand.

I immediately do the same thing and he stands. "I should go. Tomorrow will be a long day."

Walking him to the door, there's a new energy between us. An invisible force humming and it's buried in my bones. Knowing nothing more about Blaze than I did before he got here, I know I'd do just about anything to make sure I keep him, and he's not even mine.

Yet.

"Keep the ice on your thumb and take another pain killer if you need to, okay?"

"I will."

He turns to leave, but I grab his arm.

"Blaze?"

Turning back, he faces me and I motion for him to stay right there. Darting into the kitchen, I remove a sunflower from the vase and wrap a damp paper towel around the bottom before presenting it to him.

His face softens when he takes the yellow flower.

"Yellow for happiness, right? Thank you for a wonderful evening, Blaze. Can I see you again tomorrow?"

Oh my god, the precious smile he aims my way is one I want to be mine and only mine.

"I'd like that. And yes, happiness. Thank you. I'll see you at the ranch then."

Before leaving, he drops a kiss to my cheek and I'm left standing at my door with a hand on my face.

Chapter 12

Blaze

"What in god's name do you need to talk to Dan about at 4 A.M?"

"Good mornin' to you too, Martin. Is he up?"

Martin scowls and waves a hand as he goes back upstairs. I didn't call ahead, but I need to talk to Dan. He always helps me see things right.

When Dan walks down the stairs, pulling on a T-shirt with a yawn, I almost feel guilty waking him up this early.

"Do you want a coffee?" Dan asks as he passes me, rubbing his face. "Martin's not big on mornings. I hope he wasn't too snappy with you."

Dan moves around in the low light of the kitchen, getting the coffee on an hour earlier than usual. Once the pot is brewing and the eye-opening aroma of fresh coffee seeps into the air, he leans against the counter and aims his perceptive gaze my way.

"Did you sleep last night? You look like shit."

"Thanks for that. No, Martin wasn't snappy and no, I didn't sleep much."

Like Dan always does, he waits for me to speak and with a huff; I sit at the kitchen table, drumming my fingers on the worn oak surface. Dan only raises an eyebrow, so I spit out what's on my mind.

"I had a date with River last night."

Dan nods patiently.

"I kissed him."

"Blaze, it's 4 A.M. Get to the point."

"Right, right. Okay, I don't really have a point? I just needed to talk to you about it."

The coffee pot beeps and he takes two mugs down, pouring and mixing them before bringing them to the table and sitting across from me.

"What's bothering you?"

Puffing my cheeks, I voice what's been on my mind since I left River's place last night.

"I really like him. He could make me very happy, but I'm fuckin' terrified, Dan. I know he's not like Ted. Deep down, I know that. He's a good person and we have chemistry like I've never felt before. Last night I was ready to take him to bed, for fuck's sake. But... I told him I wanted to date first."

Dan sips his coffee with a shrug. "So date. And tell me the real reason you're here."

I at least have the decency to look apologetic. Dan has known me since we were kids and he's always been a no bullshit kind of guy.

"Am I good enough for him? He seems like such a tender soul and I've spent the last few years of my life locked in an office jaded and doubtin' anythin' good in the world. He told me about his mom last night and it's so night and day from my family. I worry that maybe... I don't know. Maybe I'll disappoint him. Maybe he won't like me after all when he knows where I came from."

"Are you fucking listening to yourself right now?" Dan shakes his head and leans back in his chair. "I don't even know where to start with you."

"What do you mean?"

"Your family and where you came from are nothing to be ashamed of. You made the best of a difficult situation and you rose so high above it, my friend. Second, do not mention that asshole's name here again. You're right, River is nothing like him. Nobody will be like him." His jaw clenches. "Finally, River fucking adores you already. He has for months."

"How do you know that? Was he that obvious all this time, and I missed it?"

Dan coughs and laughs as he tries to swallow, dribbling coffee down his chest and onto the table.

"Oh my god, Blaze. You really were oblivious?"

"Well, we were friendly, and I stabbed him by accident, but in my defence, he distracted me with all his... cuteness. But I never got the vibe he was interested."

"That man has been low key crushing on you since you first showed up here and took Joker for a ride. He had to pick his jaw up off the ground that day. Christ, so did I. You looked like Rip right out of that show Yellowstone, only more smiley."

"Really?"

After he takes his shirt off, giving up on saving it for the day, my friend hits me with a piece of truth. And the truth always carries a sting.

"For a smart and successful man, you really are blind to things around you. You know I love you and you're my best friend in the world, but let me tell it to you straight. Stop living afraid. Jump in. Full speed ahead. Take him on a trip. Spend all day in bed. Buy him roses every day for a month. Let him sleep over and make you breakfast. Stay up all-night binge watching a TV show. Do it all, Blaze. Don't think about not being good enough because you are. River is one of the kindest people I've ever met. Take the chance and stop thinking about all the bad that might happen, because if you keep waiting for bad, you miss all the good."

"Why am I so scared I'll fuck it all up?"

"Because you're human and you like him enough already, you're afraid to lose him. It's human nature."

Dan moves to refill our mugs as Martin walks down the stairs. He's showered and dressed in his suit already for work. The moment Dan notices he's in the kitchen with him, his whole demeanor changes. The soft look in his eyes as he winds an arm around Martin's waist and kisses his temple. Even Martin, scowly, morning Martin, leans into Dan and caresses his back. Martin tilts his head up for a kiss and the pure adoration on Dan's face as he kisses him takes my breath away. I feel like a peeping tom, but I want that. That's what I want.

I want stolen kitchen kisses and hugs.

I want barefoot in the kitchen laughing as we make breakfast together and I want someone to look at me like Dan looks at Martin.

I want that so badly my bones ache for it.

Dan and Martin are still whispering to each other, stuck at the shoulder, and I need air. Without a word, I leave the table and pull on my boots to exit to the yard. The sun is still thinking about rising and nobody has arrived for work yet. Not for at least another thirty minutes. Thinking I'll take the time to watch the sunrise and think, I cross the yard to the side of one of the horse barns where the view is best and I find Alec, the ranch foreman, already there.

"Oh, sorry. Do you mind if I join you?"

"No. It's fine."

We lean against the fence for a few minutes, lost in our thoughts before he speaks up.

"Do you mind if I ask you something?"

"As long as you're okay if I don't have an answer."

"That's fair." He peers into his coffee mug before going back to the sunrise, and even in the low light, I notice the exhaustion on his face.

"Is everything okay, Alec?"

"No? Maybe?" He huffs a laugh. "I know I'm rather quiet and not around much, but I've always been that way. Dan is the only friend I have. Well, Dante too." He glances my way. "Maybe you if you keep hanging out watching sunrises with me."

"Stranger things have happened. I've been known to watch sunrises."

We stand in silence a little longer and it's my favourite part of the day. Listening to birds sing after a long night and the rustling of forest critters waking to hurry and gather food. It's a time when my thoughts are always the loudest.

"Have you ever.... were you ever interested in a straight guy?"

"Oh yes. Tenth grade, I had the biggest crush on one of the local hockey players. I tutored him at the Boys and Girls Club and I never wanted someone to be more bi curious in my life. Sadly, I didn't get to live the dream of the athlete and nerd thing. I think he knew I liked him, too."

"So, you never acted on it?"

I shake my head. "Nope. I don't think he would have beaten me up or anything like that. But I didn't want to upset anyone, so I kept it to myself."

Alec nods in thought, focused on the sunrise. "I think I'm in love with him." He whispers. "I don't know if I should tell him or not."

"I've got a similar dilemma. You know what Dan told me? He said to go all in and if you always wait for the bad, you miss the good."

"Forget about broken hearts or shattered friendships and just do it? That's his advice?" Alec seems unsure of that, but I'm seeing it clearly.

"Yeah, pretty much. And when I came out here, I was going to think about it. But I think he's right. In my case, I let one bad relationship govern my choices for too long. But it's time to just do it. Only way I'm going to know if I've got a chance for somethin' great, you know? I don't want to spend the rest of my life wonderin' and watch him give up and move on with someone else. I want to shoot my shot."

"You must be talking about River."

"Am I seriously the only one who hasn't noticed this?"

He allows himself a smile. "Seems so." Patting my shoulder, he turns to leave. "Thanks for the talk. And good luck."

Tires crunching on the gravel in the yard tears me away from the sunrise.

Work still needs to be done.

"Now you're going to attach the ramp for the chickens here. Grab the longer nails, Heath."

River has been directing Heath and me all morning to finish the chicken coop. His thumb is a giant purple mess, but he assures me it only hurts a little. He just can't hold anything properly.

Heath takes a moment to gather the final pieces and River smiles at me while he leans on the fence post nearby.

"Are you enjoyin' tellin' us both what to do?"

He winks with a sly smile. "Maybe a little."

"Are these the right ones, River?" Heath shows the package to him and River assures him it's correct and praises him. Heath fucking beams under River's attention and I'd be jealous if I didn't know how River's lips felt against mine.

"So what we need to do is slot that ramp in the groove and attach it. Blaze and I can hold it while you do it." River motions for me to move to one side of the ramp and together we fit it in its place.

"Heath, make sure the nails are in all the way and flat. We'll cover it with the grippy stuff after. Blaze, make sure you don't drop your side."

River smirks behind Heath's back as he hammers nails in. "Firm grip, Blaze, your side is drooping."

"Oh, it's firm, no drooping here. I think it must be you."

Heath pauses and glances between us before continuing. River bites his lip, doing his best not to laugh. "Oh, it's not me."

Neither of us are paying attention to Heath and I'm really regretting my choice last night for us to take things slow.

"I'm done! We did it!" Heath steps backwards, stepping on River's foot. "Oh, shit. Sorry River."

River grimaces. "I'm okay." He claps Heath on the back. "But yes, you did it! How do you feel about carpentry now?"

"It's fun. I liked it. Can we finish the fence?"

"You know it. We need to finish it all today. Dan has chickens arriving on Monday and I have plans tonight. I don't need to be here all weekend finishing a job."

River looks at me when he says it and it's silly to think once I had the attention of this man I'd be able to take anything slow. Especially since everyone but me seems to have noticed his interest over the past few months. Dan was right. Sometimes I'm not too bright for a smart guy.

"Right, poles in holes." I say and wink back at River.

His eyes widen and he mutters under his breath as he follows Heath to the first fence pole.

Laughing, I follow along, counting down the hours until we're finished.

CHAPTER 13

RIVER

Is flirting all day at work some kind of edging torture?

I know I started it, but damn... that made for a very long day. My plans with Blaze aren't until after dinner. Friday nights, I have supper with my dad at his retirement home. I've been doing it for years and it takes a major event for me to cancel on him. Even the simmering promise of sex with Blaze is not enough for me to ditch the time with my dad.

But I need to call him and tell him I'm running late.

When he answers my call, his voice always makes me smile. Because he's never without a smile and you can hear it in his voice.

"Hi River!"

"Hey dad, I'm still coming. Just letting you know I'll be a little late. I just got in and I need to shower. You still want meatloaf from the diner tonight?"

"Oh, sure. That sounds great. I won't waste away or anything while I wait."

He laughs this little barky kind of laugh that only he can do, and I love it.

"Okay! I'll phone in our dinner now, shower and I should be there by six."

"No problem, son. See you soon."

Dad hangs up without saying goodbye. He never says goodbye. It's see you soon or you take care now. Never goodbye and I kind of like it.

Dialing the diner, I order the meatloaf for dad and fish and chips for me before I tear my clothes off and jump in the shower. After my visit with dad, I'll be meeting Blaze for the annual Fall Fling by the lake. It's a fundraiser the LGBTQ+ youth shelter organizes every year, and it's a huge local event. Bloomburg has a few celebrities that built the shelter, along with an animal shelter, and the town goes nuts to meet them and support it every year.

Fortunately, I didn't need their services, but my dad always wants to support them. He doesn't have a lot of extra money. His pension covers his residence with not much left over. I cover any of his medications that aren't paid for so he has pocket money for gifts or snacks from the little gift shop they have in his building. He saves a few dollars every month just so he can give me fifty dollars to put in their donation bin. That's the type of guy my dad is and always has been.

With a towel around my waist, I stand in front of my tiny closet, wondering what to wear. I dressed nice for our dinner date because that's what you do for something like that. But we will be outside for most of tonight and possibly dancing at the party. Is this what women go through all the time? Agonizing over their outfit? My newest pair of jeans, a black t-shirt and a hunter green button up is what I go with. Seems like it's versatile enough for the event. I think?

As long as Blaze likes how I look, that's all that matters.

Normally I slap a ball cap on, but today I'll style my hair. And by style, I mean some gel and my fingers. I rub it around my hand

and run it through my hair, taking care to make the bit of bangs I have stay in place. Kelly says it's like a superman curl so I figure why not play with it?

Making sure I have our event tickets, I rush out the door to the diner. The couple who owns the diner are such sweet people. All the food is home cooked and Char, the wife and owner, used to cook special meals for my mom when she was sick. Now when she has time, she often slips in a treat for my dad.

The jangling of bells on the diner door and the aroma of fresh roasted garlic and fried hamburger greet me when I step inside.

"Hi, River. You're looking very nice tonight."

Char carries over a takeout bag from the kitchen to me as I fish out my wallet.

"Thank you. You're looking beautiful, as always."

"Such a sweet talker you are. Who's the lucky gentleman?"

"My dad." I wink at her, and her booming laugh fills the almost empty restaurant. "How come it's so dead tonight? Isn't it busier on Fridays?"

"Just the way it is. The Fall Fling serves food and more people than ever have tickets this year. We had a late lunch crowd today, though. Are you going to the event tonight?"

"I am. Got my tickets right here." I pat my shirt pocket and she beams.

"You said tickets. You do have a date."

"I do." Stuffing my wallet back in my pants, I grab my food. "And maybe I'll tell you about it next week."

Chuckling at her expression as I leave, I place the food on the floor of the truck to get to dad's before it gets all cold and soggy. Dad won't care since it's all home cooked food and not the processed stuff he gets in this retirement home. Friday night suppers with me are when he eats the best. I've noticed he's looking a little bonier than usual, too. I should ask the workers how he eats during the week.

After signing in and chatting with the ladies at the front desk, I head down the hall to dad's room and let myself in.

"Hi, dad! I'm here!"

He grabs the remote, turning the TV off and beams his giant smile my way.

"Well, don't you look nice, son. Where are you off to tonight?"

He shuffles over with his walker to the tiny two-seater table and eases himself in his chair. Placing plates and cutlery down, I serve dad his dinner first before plating mine and joining him.

"The Fall Fling is tonight. I got tickets from Dan's boyfriend, Martin. The brewery supplies the beer, and they had tickets to give away, so I accepted."

Dad separates his potatoes and carrots from the meatloaf and adds more ketchup to it before he even takes a bite.

"And you're taking a friend?"

Nodding, I chew a fry before answering. "I am. His name is Blaze. It's our second date."

"Your second! When was the first?"

My cheeks heat as I cut my fish. "Last night, actually."

"So. What's he like? Tell me about him."

Dad is excited, and before I tell him about Blaze, I realize I am, too. A buzzing in my gut started when I was still in the shower and it's still there. And it's not just because he's a gorgeous man. He's tender and kind, thoughtful and a little mysterious. He's definitely a whole lot of sexy because I'm obsessed with kissing him again. Maybe even more than kissing.

"We work together at the ranch. Remember, I told you he's the one who helped Colby with his store?"

"Oh! The same guy who wore a suit that day and you didn't recognize him?"

He shovels more meatloaf in his mouth and I laugh.

"Yup. Same guy. He's really sweet, Dad. I mean, we're attracted to each other. But he's very... guarded. Almost like he's protective of his feelings, you know? I think he's scared of us going too fast because he said he's old-fashioned and wants to date before we fall into bed. But..."

I pause since I was on the verge of telling my dad how hot Blaze makes me, but I should have known dad would already be onto it. His smile couldn't be any more mischievous.

"Don't worry, son. I know that look and I may be old, but I remember how it feels when your body lights up for someone. When I first met your mother, I wanted to pick her an entire field of wildflowers to earn that first kiss. But I also wouldn't have said no if she said don't bother and got naked either."

"Dad!" I choke on my fish and take a drink of water. "I don't need the image of you and mom naked in a field of wildflowers before my date, thank you."

"So, you don't want slow then? It's only your second date and you want more? Spell it out for me."

Blaze has been under my skin in the best kind of way since he first arrived at the ranch. All dark and mysterious, with his aviator glasses and smooth beard. His confidence when he rode the horse named Joker nobody else would ride because he was unpredictable. And most recently, his kindness towards Colby and Dante when they needed a small miracle. Not only did he reveal he was a very rich man to everyone by doing it, he showed us how loyal he is to people in his life.

Honestly, that's the biggest turn on of all. I've seen it with Dan, but I didn't think Blaze extended that level of commitment to everyone in his life.

I still don't know what makes Blaze tick. I want to find out, but I don't want to go slow.

"I want him all now, Dad. It's that simple. But I respect his wishes because I think he's worried about a broken heart. I'm only guessing, but I think he might also be concerned once people know he has money, that's all they see. He's keeping a safe distance for now."

"Everyone worries about broken hearts. It happens. Maybe he thinks sex too soon won't let him see red flags if you were into him only for money. Not that you would be, of course."

Sighing, I sit back. No longer hungry.

"He said something last night. He said he had emotional scars and then changed the subject after I told him about mom. He knows why the workshop is so special. I gave him a lesson there and he picked up on my vibes. We were already growing close, and I felt like we had a connection, so I spilled that story all out."

"And he didn't want to share his own?"

Shrugging, I clear off the table. "I think he did, but then I asked him to kiss me and we never got back to it."

Dad chuckles with a shake of his head. "You get your directness from your mother."

"It comes in handy sometimes." I laugh and dad joins in. "He'll tell me when he's ready, is my guess, and I really like him. It's been years since I've even had a sliver of interest in anyone. Blaze has been in my head since the day I met him."

Dad moves back to his recliner and I wash up our few dishes, making sure his tiny kitchenette space is as clean as it should be. My next visit, I'll be sure to restock his snacks and drinks.

"If you want my advice, I say tell him how you feel right away. Don't give him any chance to get all up in his head wondering where you stand. If it's just sex, tell him. If you're looking for a partner and more than just a roll in the sheets, tell him that too. Life is too short to be left wondering where you stand. And nobody needs games."

"Wise words, Dad. I don't have an issue with being direct. We've established that."

Dad flicks the TV back on and as we always do on Fridays we have the news on mute and chat about local news and anything that happened in the world. I tell him about my carving and furniture projects. He listens and shares stories of when he and mom were young. It's my favourite night of the week. Dad will be eighty-five next year and life is too precious to not savour all these moments. The older I've grown, the more I've enjoyed our talks and listening to him. Knowing they will end at some point makes me sad, so I want as many as I can.

"Son, it's getting towards eight o'clock. Go meet your date." He unfolds a paper cheque from his pocket. "Give this to the lads for me? Tell them I'm happy they're here for the youth who need them."

Leaning down, I give him a hug and a kiss, a little teary at his gesture.

"Goodnight. I'll definitely do that. Love you, dad."

"Take care, son."

Signing out of his building, I slip behind the wheel of my truck. Before I drive, I send Blaze a text.

River: Just leaving dad's. I'll be at your place in about twenty minutes.

Blaze: Looking forward to it.

CHAPTER 14

BLAZE

If I fix my hair or change my shirt one more time, I'll officially be too damn nervous to leave the house. I don't even know why I'm nervous. It's a date with River. My second one if I want to get technical about it.

And the first one was one of the most memorable nights of my life. My gaze lands on the sunflower in the mason jar I placed on my dining room table. I hope he didn't notice how I almost teared up when he handed that flower to me. Something so small shouldn't have me feeling so jumbled up.

But I asked for romance and he listened.

Maybe that's my issue. The fact he listened and actually acted on my request. Nobody has even done that before.

MEOW

My cat, Mando, agrees with my inner turmoil, but needs an ear scratch regardless of my mood.

"Thanks, buddy. I know it's not easy livin' with me sometimes."

The doorbell sounds and for one fleeting moment I consider changing my mind, but Dan's words about missing out on the good tumble around my brain. I won't miss out on good anymore. With a steadying breath, I open the door to a sight that makes my knees wobble.

River stands there, dressed in casual jeans and probably his favourite button-up shirt if the faded cuffs are anything to go by. Even with the chill in the early October evening, he's opted for no jacket. He styled his brown hair, probably with as much effort as mine, if the curl on his forehead is a clue to the amount of hair product he's used.

But in addition to his cute and casual appearance he's holding a fucking bouquet of flowers.

Not just any flowers. Tulips. Red tulips, a spring flower to represent passion, that he's somehow found for me completely out of season.

"Hi. These are for you."

Thrusting them towards me, I finally shake my head and invite him in while accepting his gift.

"Thank you. How did you find tulips in the fall?" My voice wavers, but I hope he doesn't notice.

Bringing them to my nose I inhale their light scent and touch a petal with a soft finger.

River swallows and he whispers, "I asked the florist in town for a favour. I wanted to get you something to brighten your day and they told me red ones were romantic. You said they were your favourite."

MEOW!

Mando rushes River's legs, weaving in and out as he waits by my front door. Crouching down, he scratches him under the chin and the cat loves it, rolling over for a tummy scratch too.

"Aren't you the cutest thing?" He croons to my cat and I'm still staring at him, mouth agape with flowers in my hand. Shit, I need to get a grip here.

"That's Mando. Let me put these in water and then we can leave."

Opening the cupboard doors in my kitchen, I discover I own exactly one vase and after shaking the flower food into the water; I place the tulips inside. I don't think anyone has ever brought me flowers. Come to think of it, I don't think I've ever had someone come and pick me up for a date, either. It's always been me doing all those things.

He brought me tulips in October.

"How long have you had your cat? He's adorable." River calls from the entrance and I'm snapped back to reality.

"Just over a year now. A few months after I moved in, I found him under the deck one mornin'. I'm guessin' someone dumped him. The vet said he was only about six weeks old when I finally caught him so I could get him looked at."

"Aww, poor guy. He seems pretty happy to be here."

With a final scratch, River straightens up to his full height again and his warm, easy smile makes the ache in my chest bloom.

"You look nice, by the way. I like your hair."

Oh, my god I sound like such a tool.

River glows and leans in to kiss my cheek. "Thank you. You don't look so bad yourself." He jams his hands in his pockets and holds up one of his booted feet. "Wear something comfy for dancing tonight."

"I thought you were takin' me to a fundraiser." I sit on the hall bench and pull on a pair of Timberlands.

"Oh, I am. And they have music and dancing starts in about an hour. It's a fun time. Most of the town seems to drop by at some point."

The way his gaze tracks my body, the smiling eyes and the lick of his lips, it all sets my heart racing. Dancing and meeting most of the town on his arm? Holy fuck, I'm all in for that.

Grabbing my wallet and keys, I say goodbye to Mando and make sure I leave the TV on with low music for him.

"Okay, let's cut a rug."

River laughs as he opens the truck door for me. "You're not ninety. Nobody talks like that. Like, nobody and my dad is almost ninety, so I know this."

I slide into the passenger seat with a laugh as he rounds to his side, still laughing.

"How about bump and grind? Is that better? Less old soundin'?"

He backs us out of my driveway, still shaking his head with a chuckle.

"We're going out, Blaze. And we're dancing. Let's just say that."

My damn smile just about breaks my face. "Right. We're goin' out. It's a date."

He reaches over to take my hand and kisses the back of it.

"It's a date."

"I want you to meet someone."

River speaks next to my ear so I can hear and I nod as he takes my hand and pulls me to a group of men standing in the corner.

We haven't been here that long, but already River has talked and introduced me to so many people I've lost count. He knows, well, he knows everyone.

He taps a shorter man with short brown hair and a slender build on the shoulder. When the man discovers it's River, he folds him into a hug.

"Hey River! Thanks for coming by. It's always nice to see you here." He gestures to the silent auction table in the corner. "Your piece is drawing lots of bids. Thank you so much for that."

"Wonderful! I was hoping it would. I tried something new, so I'm glad people like it." He pulls a paper from his pocket and hands it to the man. "Dad sends his thanks to you and the rest of the lads for operating the shelter."

"Ah, he's so sweet. Tell him we thank him so much."

River reaches for me again and pulls me forward. "Jake, this is Blaze. I don't think you've officially met."

Jake holds out his hand and I accept it. "I've seen you at the brewery with Dan a few times, right? Martin works with my boyfriend." He points to a mountain of blond muscle a few feet away. "Dan helps Matts with planting for them. You've probably seen Matts a few times."

"I have yes, and you look familiar. I haven't got out too much since moving here. But it's nice to meet you. River tells me this event gets bigger every year and you organize it all yourself."

Jake dips his head, a slight blush on his cheeks. "It's a passion project and I'm very proud of it. Thank you for coming." He waves at someone over River's shoulder. "I gotta take care of something. If you see my brother, make sure you say hello." He pats my arm.

"It's so wonderful to meet you. Enjoy your time with River." He leans in close. "He's a sweet, sweet man. You're very lucky."

Jake rushes off and River laces his fingers back through mine, tugging me over to the table of auction items.

"Let me show you what I made for them."

The crowd at the auction table isn't very large and he stops in the middle. He doesn't need to say anything else because I think I gasp when I see what can only be River's donation to the auction.

He carved a fucking statue. And it's breathtaking.

Reaching out to touch it, I pull my hand back. "Am I allowed to touch it?"

"I'm right here. I won't let them kick you out." He winks and motions for me to go ahead. I can't explain why I want to. I just have to.

I don't know what kind of wood he used, I'm no expert on materials that way. But the piece is heart-shaped and inside the heart is a person. It has no identifiable gender and facial features. On one side of the person is a dog and a cat. Again, there's no gender noticeable on the animals either and no faces. Even without identifying features, it's intricate and detailed, but it's the inscription carved and painted that draws my eye.

Love has no face, only heart.

"Do you like it?"

River's breath next to my ear sends shivers racing across my skin.

"It's amazin'. You're amazin'. River... I'm breathless over this." Searching the table for a pen, I find the paper to bid and pause before I do. Searching his face, I ask, "I can bid on it right? You're okay with that?"

"It's for charity. Anyone can bid."

I know I can drop an obscene amount of money right now and nobody would match it. But I also have to leave my name and number. It's what I hate about these kinds of things. I bid the next person up by $50 and drop the pen.

"Make sure we come back here before we leave. I want to win something."

His hand rests on my hip as he presses a kiss to the corner of my mouth. "Oh, I think you'll win something by the time we leave here."

My lips try to catch his before he draws away, but he grins back. "First we dance, Blaze. Let's, what do you call it? Cut a rug?" He snorts as he leads me out to the covered tent for dancing.

"Are you always going to tease me about that?"

"Maybe? Depends if you can dance or not?"

The music playing is not something for the younger crowd. Like any event, they play music for the older couples who are usually in bed by nine, and this is their time to whoop it up. But what River doesn't know is I took dance lessons.

Pulling him into me, I slide into a fast waltz with ease, leading him through the steps, but the pressure on my hand signals he also knows what he's doing here.

"Do you know how to formally ballroom dance, Mr.McAdam s?"

"You're not the only one with secrets, Mr.Porter. But I prefer to lead, if you don't mind."

With a swallow, I stare at his handsome face with his wicked grin and, not for the first time tonight, I wish I hadn't closed myself off from him when I first got here. Our steps stutter as I drop my pressure on his back and lead hand and allow him to take over. It's the first time I've ever danced with someone and not had to lead.

It's a weird feeling, but River's hand shifts occasionally on the small of my back and while it's firm, it's also gentle and I find myself melting into him.

"How did you learn how to dance?" He asks as the music slows and we adjust our paces.

"It's a shit story. I hired someone to help me with my public image. He suggested dancin' would help me blend in with the business crowd."

Because I was a backwoods boy with no social skills and a tendency to drop my "ings" he also suggested speech lessons. Which I took even though I died a little inside.

"Well, I don't think anyone should just blend in. Ever."

I'm starting to learn that. Better late than never, I suppose.

"What about you? How does a master carver and furniture builder know how to waltz?"

River's lips tilt as he leads us into a fast twirl. I snort out a laugh at how easy he did that and how fucking good it feels to let loose and just be me with him.

"My best friend wanted to learn and didn't want to go by herself, so I went with her. Turns out she's not very good at it, but I am." He winks and presses his cheek into mine, his lips ghosting over my ear. "I can also tango very well should you ever want to do that with me."

Our lower bodies press together as he moves me at his will through the crowd of other dancers. Although I'm only vaguely aware of other people around. I'm caught in the spell of River and I'd do just about anything to stay here.

"Tango is the dance of love, is it not?"

I smile against his ear when he misses a step but recovers.

"It is. But it's also trust. Trusting your partner to not let go, to catch you when needed." The music ends, and the DJ is announcing a short break to switch to modern music, as he calls it. But River doesn't let go right away. His breath still skates over my skin near my neck and his hand splayed on my back, brands my skin through my shirt.

Reluctantly, we put space between us as someone bumps us on the way by.

"Do you want to get a drink?" I ask, because it's the only thing I trust myself saying.

"Of course. Are you having fun?"

Laughing, I kiss him on the cheek. "I somehow think there's never a borin' time with you."

Waving down the bartender, he orders himself a water and waits for my request. "Anything in a can is fine."

River hands the guy money and motions for a quiet corner in the tent where we can talk at a high table.

"Can I ask you what you meant when you said you had a PR guy tell you to learn how to dance? I feel like that's maybe something you might not want to tell me, but I'd still like to ask."

Rolling the can between by palms, I choose my words before telling River.

"So you know, I kind of just showed up at the ranch one day, right?" He nods. "It wasn't a decision I made easily or lightly. When I built that company, it meant the world to me."

Pausing, I scan River's face. He's listening and the warmth there is one to trust. I know this. But one thing at a time.

"I may have grown up here with Dan, but I didn't have what you'd call a palatable home life and history. Early on I met a man named Ted." Taking a swallow of beer, I gather my words. "He was beautiful. He swept me off my feet." I laugh softly. "I had just made a leap into the big market and scored my first major client. I had more money in one week than I'd ever seen in my life. Heather and I upgraded our offices. I bought a new suit, and I met Ted."

"Hey, you don't have to get into it, Blaze. If it's too hard for you, don't talk. I want tonight to be for us and be happy."

River peels my hand off the beer can and curls his fingers around it. "We've got lots of time to learn the painful shit about each other. Let's enjoy tonight."

Squeezing his hand back, I didn't think it would be so hard to tell him about Ted. "Right. Let's enjoy the night. I want to tell you the whole story, though."

"And I'll be there to hold you when you do." Bringing my hand to his lips, he kisses my knuckles and the sweet gesture has me slam my eyes closed. River might be the one to hold my heart and while it's what I want, it scares the shit out of me.

CHAPTER 15

RIVER

B laze is a beautiful riddle.

He's always so confident and carries an aura of respect you can't ignore if you tried. He has a large personality, and he's so very easy to like. But it's not who he really is. He's a marshmallow with a broken heart that he's still doing his damndest to protect. He didn't need to tell me anything else about Ted. I know where it's going. Those stories never end well. Hell, I have a few of my own, but they don't stick to me as much as Blaze's story does.

The night is growing late and most of the dancers have cleared out now, leaving a handful of drunken revelers behind. Blaze ran off to the restroom and while I chug another bottle of water, someone joins me in my space.

"Great night, isn't it? I love coming to these."

"Hey, Zane. I didn't see you earlier. Are you here by yourself?"

Zane is an owner of the brewery with Dan's boyfriend Martin. He's been around the ranch a fair bit and while I know who he is, I don't really know him. Well, I know one thing. Zane is an eternal ray of sunshine.

"Huh, I guess I am." He laughs. "Martin left after dinner. Matts already left with Jake and Dylan couldn't come. So I've just been wandering around dancing with people."

Leaning on the table, his relaxed smile says he has zero issues being here by himself too. It's just Zane, the ultimate extrovert, making friends in every corner.

"Word at the ranch is you and Blaze are getting cozy. I saw you guys dancing." He wiggles his eyebrows and I shake my head at his sunshine grin. "Although if there was no talk before, there would be after tonight. I don't think you two noticed the audience you had most of the time. You two are fire, though." He leans in to whisper, "And I'm not even gay."

"We're dating, yes. He's a great guy."

"Who's a great guy?" Blaze shows up behind me, wrapping his arms around my waist and resting his chin on my shoulder.

"Awww... look at you two." Zane clasps his hands against his heart with a smile. "Aren't you so freaking adorbs, as my niece would say."

Blaze nuzzles his face into my neck and walks his lips up my neck and I forget Zane is there. But for only like two seconds, maybe four. Then I open my eyes to see him backing away from us, shaking his finger like we're naughty children with a giant smile.

"Can we go now?" Blaze's voice rumbles in my ear.

"Did I just go mute in front of Zane?"

"Yes, right after you groaned like a porn star."

"I did not!" I gasp.

Blaze allows me to spin in his arms and he rests his hands on my waist.

"You did actually. It was hot. Zane just snorted and started backin' away. He's not offended, but don't be surprised if he teases you later."

"You want me to take you home?"

Blaze's eyes soften as he slides his hands up my arms. "Please."

I'd likely do anything he ever asked of me. Even if the word please didn't sound like a promise from his lips.

The only good thing about this date ending is the possibility of something else starting in its place.

Blaze got out of his side of the truck before I could come around and open the door for him. He probably would've stayed and let me open the door for him if I asked him to, but I'll have to settle for walking him up to his door instead.

"Thank you for a great night out, Blaze."

As we walk to his door, the moon is high, and it lights our way up his porch steps. When he left the city, he went all in. His ranch style bungalow couldn't be more secluded. There are several farms within sight, but nothing close, not even a streetlight. The privacy here is intimate in the rustic way only country life can bring.

"River, I had one of the best times of my life tonight. I don't want it to end."

"Okay, then don't."

If he doesn't say it, I will, but I really want him to first. He's the one who asked for romance and slow dating and I'll do that always if it's what he wants. But I really hope after our time together tonight he changes his mind on the slow part. So much so that I wish I kept my lucky rabbit's foot in my pocket.

After turning the key in the lock, he keeps his hand on the door handle. I stand a step away to give him space. If all he wants is a good-night kiss at the door, then I'll do it and rush home to take matters into my own hands.

"Would you like to come in for... I'd say a drink, but that's too cheesy even for me. But... can you come in?"

"I'd like that."

Once inside, Mando trots up to greet us with several meows. He chirps and purrs until Blaze scoops him into his arms for a hug and an ear scratch before setting him back down and Mando trots away, pleased with the affection.

"Heh, he has to have a snuggle first thing, or he'll never give me a moment of peace."

Blaze dips his head, like he's embarrassed to tell me that, and I laugh softly.

"I can't say that I blame him. Smart cat."

"Thank you."

And the man blushes. After everything I've said and done, that's what makes him blush?

Perhaps words hit differently since we're in his home and this is the space he can just be himself. Whatever it is, I'm not complaining and I still side with the cat. Lucky bastard.

"Um, so, can I get you anythin'?"

"Just you next to me on the couch, if that's a choice I can have."

Blaze's eyes widen but he nods, and motions me to his living room. It's tastefully decorated with a couch similar to mine, soft and comfortable, just not as wide. A gas fireplace sits under the flat screen television that's mounted on the wall and off to the side is a smaller TV on the floor. Just a tiny flatscreen with feet and its own cable box.

Taking a seat on the end of the couch, I drape my arm across the back with the invitation to take the seat next to me. With a smile he does and he brings the remote control with him.

"What's the small TV on the floor for?"

"Oh, that's for Mando."

"You got the cat his own TV? That's a little over the top there, Blaze. Even for a rich guy."

He turns to me, a smirk on his gorgeous face and the crinkling lines around his eyes make my knees weak. God, how did I keep away from him this long?

"He was jumpin' up over the fireplace to swat at the animals on TV. I was worried he'd fall and burn his paws on the fireplace or somethin' worse if he fell. I wouldn't be able to live with myself if he pulled the TV down with him. So I got him his own and he can't hurt himself now." He leans into my side and there's nothing more perfect than this moment. Just two men, snuggling on the couch and talking about a pet. If I didn't know I longed for this kind of domestic comfort before, I sure do now.

"So what does he like to watch?"

Blaze snorts. "Meerkat Manor and curling. Those are his favourites."

My body shakes with laughter. "He watches curling?"

He smiles back at me and my breath catches. Fuck, his eyes are gorgeous this close. Shining like two sapphires or some other poetic crap. I'm a romantic with actions, not words.

"He does! Even gets his paws up there to catch the rock some-times. It's like he wants to sweep and it's super adorable."

Blaze raises the remote, but I swipe it out of his hand.

"I don't want to watch TV, Blaze." My voice is guttural, scratchy and for a hot minute I wonder if it was actually me that said those words. This is it. If he says no, then I'll respect that.

"What do ya want, darlin'?"

Swallowing, I tip up his chin with my fingertips.

"I know you said you wanted slow romance and getting to know each other, but Jesus Christ, Blaze. I'm a man fighting to keep myself from begging you to get naked and making you come with my name on your lips."

The rapid rise of his chest and his tongue licking his lips, like he's savouring my words, almost do me in.

"Okay."

"What's okay? Are we on the same page, Blaze? Are you on board to move this thing with us to the next level?"

Dear god, his eyes. They're telling me wicked things, but I need his mouth to catch up.

"Yeah, but I don't want a page. Let's start a chapter."

Blaze leans forward, his lips smashing into mine with such ago-nizing sweetness I hope he can't feel my heart clawing its way out of my chest. It's not just been the last few days, but ever since he set foot here, I've wanted this. No, not just wanted it, but dreamed about it.

Hands roam as we kiss and try to undress each other in the most clumsy of fashion. Bumping noses and fumbling fingers on buttons and zippers. With a burst of giggles, it reminds me of the time I lost my virginity.

"Why are you laughin'?" Blaze pulls away with a raised eyebrow. "If my dick was out right now, I'd be very offended."

That just makes me laugh harder.

"I was just thinking of how awkward we are and all the bumping and fumbling. It reminded me of when I lost my virginity. It was so, so awkward and bad."

"I don't know if you're aware, but talkin' about a time you had bad sex when you're about to have sex with someone new is not recommended."

Blaze's dry tone only spurs more laughs. "Oh god. I'm such a loser. I didn't mean to imply anything. It was just... I mean...," Sucking in a breath, I motion between us. "We aren't going to be bad together. Not even close. We're just clumsy as hell and so out of practice. Shit, did I ruin the mood?"

When he snorts and shakes his head no, I send a silent prayer of thank you to whatever deity might be listening that this guy is amazing.

"I don't remember the last time I laughed when I'm tryin' to get in a guy's pants. Maybe never."

His eyebrows squinch in thought. "I guess that makes this a first for me."

Without our lips and bodies fused together, Blaze leans back and finishes the final buttons so he can fling his shirt off and he reaches to finish mine.

"What's a first for you?" I ask with a breathy sigh as he helps me out of my clothes.

"To feel so secure and perfect with someone that I can laugh when my dick is pressin' so hard into my zipper, it's painful. And that you won't judge me for being even a little awkward."

Blaze's words are pure and from the heart. When his fingers dance over the bulge in my pants to reach the button, he pauses and sets those brilliant blues on me. "That I feel safe enough to be me with you."

"I don't want you to be anything but you, Blaze."

Surging up, I cradle his face in my hands. "You're almost perfect, just as you are." I feather kisses across his jaw and back to his lips.

"Almost perfect?" He murmurs when my lips meet his.

"You'll be completely perfect when you let me make you come, but not until then."

"Okay then, make me perfect darlin'"

Slipping off the couch, I kneel between his legs as he lifts his hips and helps me remove his pants. I struggle when they get stuck at his ankles and I growl, giving up on the second one and leaving it knotted there.

"You in a hurry?" Blaze drawls as he widens his legs and trails his hand up his chest. Those eyes are going to kill me. Or his muscular legs one day when he wraps them around me. Either way, I'll die happy.

Tucking my fingers into the band of his boxers, I pin him with a stare. "A hurry to see you naked, yes. A hurry for this to be over? Fuck no."

He lifts his hips again and I slide the final piece of clothing off and, just like that, Blaze is naked before me. His cock leaks as I drink my fill of him. Blaze seems to enjoy me only looking without touching. One hand roams his chest and the other one strokes his cock with a lazy hand. His blue eyes might as well be on fire because my skin feels far too hot with his gaze focused on me.

Too fast I shimmy out of my pants and almost fall over, catching myself on the arm of the couch before I crash in epic form.

"Smooth." Blaze barks with a laugh.

"You should take it as a compliment. It shows how eager I am."

"I appreciate the extra effort. Makes a guy feel wanted."

He says those words in his lazy drawl, but I hear what he left out. He hasn't filled me in on everything about this Ted guy, but whatever happened fucked with his confidence in the bedroom. Blaze feels less than with his clothes off and I hope I can help him understand that he's anything but.

"Good, because I've wanted you for some time now." I strip off my boxers and make sure he notices how damn hard I am for him before I step back between his legs. "This is what you do to me. Clothes on or off I want you."

I sink to my knees and with no more damn talking; I lick a stripe up his dick before taking him as far as I can in one swallow. He's a lot bigger than I estimated now that he's in my mouth and he almost breaks my nose when he shoots his hips up.

"Jesus, River. A little warnin' next time that you don't move slow." He pants and drops his head back against the sofa with a groan.

"You almost broke my nose." I laugh and when he lifts his head to peer down at me with his lust filled eyes, the laugh dies in my throat.

"Stop talkin' darlin'. Make good on your promise and make me come."

This time he at least stays put, and when I stretch my jaw around him, I'm rewarded with a low growl and the sweet sound of my name on his lips.

I'm not a blushing virgin or anything. I've been with other men before, but Blaze is so different. From the way he smiles at a bouquet of flowers to how the weight of his dick feels on my tongue. He's just a step above anyone else. Like the top shelf liquor or fine wine, he offers a higher experience.

Cupping his balls with one hand, I double down my effort to take more of him in my mouth.

"River... fuck, just like that."

He already sounds wrecked and my lust-addled brain skips ahead to what it will be like to have sex. Or to have him worship me in the same way. Dear lord, I want that. I want everything.

Peering up, I find Blaze's gaze still pinned on me as his fingers dust across his pebbled nipples.

"So close... "

He trails off and his mouth falls slack before a low moan escapes his lips.

"Say my name, Blaze." My voice is hoarse when I switch my mouth with my hand, but he somehow follows my request.

"River... "

His dick spills cum over his stomach and into my hand as I stroke him through his orgasm. He's now officially fucking perfect.

"River... "

When he opens his eyes, his lips tilt in a sex drunk kinda way. He licks his lips as his gaze darts to the mess on my hand. Bringing my hand to my mouth, I lick it off before pressing my lips to his and he devours my mouth. It's everything he keeps inside, broken open with the intimacy of a moment that was maybe only supposed to be about sex, but turned into a lot more and it leaves me breathless.

It won't take long for me to come. I've been on a hair trigger since I got him naked and now he's writhing under me, panting and so damn... vulnerable.

"When did you last jack off? There's enough spluge here for me to be concerned for your well being. Sperm retention syndrome is a thing."

"Stop talkin' and come on me, darlin'."

I wrap my hand, still slick with his spunk, around my cock. His gaze locks on my hand as I jerk myself on top of him and do as he asks. Fuck, I'll do anything he asks.

"Fuck... yessss... "

Gasping, I empty on him and his lips tilt in a sexy smirk as I try to catch my breath.

"Jesus, Blaze. What the hell just happened?"

Lounging back, like he wants to drift off to sleep, he raises a hand to my face. He runs his thumb along my jaw before carefully sitting up to plant a tender kiss on my lips.

"What I hope is the start of a new chapter."

CHAPTER 16

BLAZE

"So, I have a great idea."

Martin begins and the rest of us groan. We've all gathered in Dan's farmhouse for an informal group get together. Dan likes to have us all together like this. It's his way of making us feel like the motley family unit we are.

And I love it. I won't say it out loud, but it's some of my favourite memories over the last year.

"It *is* a good idea! Listen, Dan already likes it, so at this point you all just have to nod and smile because we're doing it."

Dan hugs Martin from behind and places a wet smack on his cheek.

"It's true. It's a great idea for the ranch, so listen to what he has to say."

Dan tops up my glass with a spiked apple cider Martin brought us from the brewery before sitting next to me while Martin speaks to the group.

"Did you ever think he'd be dreaming up stuff for the ranch that involved him getting dirty?" Dan speaks low next to my ear and I hold in a laugh.

"Never in a million years." I listen as Martin flaps his hands and gestures like he's playing charades. A sideways glance at Dan has me shaking my head. "Would you stop with all the heart eyes. I'm gonna be sick."

Dan sticks out his tongue. "You're one to talk. You've been mooning over River every chance you get."

He's got me there. While I teased Dan frequently about falling in love and being so sweet on him, I can't do that anymore. Because he's right.

Since River took me to the fundraiser on our first official date, he's all I can think about. If he's not working with me, I seek him out. If he's across the room like he is now laughing with Dante, my eyes will find him.

Every. Single. Time.

"I can't even deny it. It's true."

"Is it going well?"

Turning to Dan, I lower my voice. We're supposed to be listening and setting an example, but this is an informal gathering. Someone can fill me in later if I miss anything. Probably Martin, since he's all about the details.

"Amazin'. I don't think I've ever felt this free."

"I've noticed you sound like the Blaze I knew before, and you carry yourself differently. You're letting him in and it looks good on you."

"He's definitely found his way behind all the barriers I had up. I'm not sure how he did, but I'm grateful."

Martin winds up and looks over to Dan and I. "Well? I think I covered it all. What do you think?"

Heath pipes up. "So you want the ranch to offer sleigh rides for the coming winter to the public on weekends or to hire for corporate events and parties? We'd build a permanent bonfire ring and shelter in the far field for hot chocolate and smores and a chance to rest the horses. The horses will benefit because it gives them the job they love and it would provide revenue for the ranch." He tilts his head. "Oh! And you've already marketed it and we have bookings."

Heath smiles at us. "I think that's all."

Thank god for Heath and his summaries since I clearly wasn't listening.

"You left out the part that Martin needs to wear rubber boots and come along a few times." I add with a snort. I'll never miss an opportunity to tease Martin.

"Must you always mock the boots? You used to be a snappily dressed business man. Doesn't it bother you not wearing your finest every day?"

I laugh. "It's not fuckin' church, Marty. And this is my business dress these days. I can't say I hate it."

Which is true. The longer I've been here and allowed myself to slip back into my old ways, the easier it's been to forget it.

"Do you ever miss it?" River asks from the other side of the room. "Your suits and the lights of the big city, I mean."

"Honestly, the only thing I miss is my friend Heather. I don't miss workin' just to make more money." River's eyes widen and I back track. "I don't mean it like that. That sounds snotty. What I mean is there was no need to keep workin' sixteen-hour days and to put my life on the back burner. The time had come for me to find a better balance. A better life. A reason to enjoy livin'."

My eyes never waver from River's and he tips his head with a tap to his chest, acknowledging what I didn't say out loud. That it's him who's shown me what I've been missing. He's not just shown me, he's taking me on a guided tour and there's not been a single minute I've wished I were doing something else.

"What about the city food? Don't you miss that?" Heath asks as he digs into the bag of chips on the table. The guy always eats, I swear.

"It was nice to have more options, but I don't miss it, no. So far I've found everythin' I need here and I'm happy."

"Indeed." Dan mumbles.

I ignore him and shove the chip bag closer to Heath.

"So was Heather your girlfriend or something?" Heath asks as he shovels more chips in his mouth. Daisy, Dan's dog, moves closer to him and lays under his chair.

"Uh... no. I've never had a girlfriend. She was the first person I hired as an assistant and she helped me build my business. She's a really close friend, much like Dan is."

"How do you never have a girlfriend and be forty? That's bizarre. God, I can't tell you how many girlfriends I've had."

Martin clears his throat and Dan stands to embrace him with a kiss to the temple. I tilt my head and wait for Heath to catch up, but it's taking far too long for him to connect the dots.

"Because I'm gay, Heath."

He blinks. Shoves more chips in his mouth and blinks again.

"I had no idea."

Even watching me and River flirt for several days, he still didn't figure it out.

"I don't wear a sign so... " I drawl and River snorts from his corner.

"Well, the bar downtown has male stripper nights if you're ever into that."

Martin smacks him on the shoulder. "He doesn't need to watch strippers, Heath. He can meet people just fine elsewhere." He turns to Dan, "Although if they ever have those gay dudes who take it all off, we should go."

Dan nods. "Sure, Marty. Whatever you say."

We discuss Martin's sleigh ride in more detail. I naturally fall into the business talk part of it and ask Dan to get me a paper and pencil so we can visualize numbers. Heath and a few others excuse themselves and it leaves Dan, Martin, River and I.

"Hey, where's Alec been? Shouldn't he be here?"

"Uh...," Martin rushes to the front window before returning. "His truck isn't here. I think he was helping Zane with something tonight. We can catch him tomorrow."

We all share ideas, and I scribble down projections on a paper. The guys share visions of how this could increase the ranch's visibility and launch a new side business. It's exhilarating to be in this kind of brainstorming activity again and it's a new sense of fulfillment. A dying spark brought back to life.

"If you don't mind, I'd love to donate the sleigh and not take it out of the workin' capital." I ask the room, but Dan is really the one who has any say in the matter.

"There's a guy in the next town over who builds them from scratch. He does great work. If you want to take a road trip with me, we could have one here before it snows." River offers.

A road trip with River? I'm not turning that down.

"Of course! I'd love to keep it local if we could."

"If he could sell us a sleigh before next month, it would ease his mind. His wife has been sick and they've fallen behind on bills. It's their main income."

Visions of my childhood come to mind, and I shake my head to clear them. "Do they have kids?"

He nods. "Two. Abby is ten and Arthur is eight." River stands. "We can talk about it tomorrow, though. I have to get to Dad's tonight and I need to run." Walking him to the door, I take him in my arms and bend to kiss his neck.

"I'll miss you tonight."

He pulls aways and lays a kiss on my lips.

"I'll text you when I get home and we'll go see the sleigh tomorrow?"

Rubbing my nose next to his, I place another kiss on his lips. "I'd love to go tomorrow. Text me. Call me. Hell, sext me if you want. And say hi to your dad for me."

"Did you just talk about my dad and sexts in the same sentence?"

"Huh. Guess I did. Sorry?"

"You might be if I can't sext now."

"Oh, darlin' don't be like that."

River laughs with another kiss and calls out a final goodbye to Dan and Martin.

Martin excuses himself with a yawn shortly after, and Dan grins at me. The same grin he had when we were kids and he had something big to share.

"That was awful sweet for a guy who has mocked me for the last year about being in love."

With a shrug, I return to my chair. "Sorry?" I laugh and Dan leans back.

"I mean it, Blaze. We haven't had time to talk much in the past few weeks. I've noticed a drastic change in you. All good. I'm so damn happy to see you happy."

"He's... special. I've met nobody like him before. River is, well, he's... probably my person."

Dan hums under his breath before reaching over to pat my shoulder.

"He's very special. One of a kind and I hope he's what you've been looking for."

"Time will tell, I guess. But right now, it's great to have someone who gets me and doesn't question why I left all the glamour of the city behind." I run a hand down my face. "Which is a lot bigger of a deal than I thought. When he asked if I missed it tonight, I think it was just a reaction, you know? He's asked me other things, but never specifically what made me leave."

Dan laughs softly. "Are you even sure you have an answer to that yourself?"

"Not really, but I like to do things backwards, don't I?"

"Cheers to that." Dan extends his cup and we toast. "Life is always a mystery. People come and people go. You keep thinking you know what you want or maybe you have what you want and then it throws something completely different at you." His gaze slides to the stairs where Martin disappeared earlier. "You gotta be ready to swing at the curve balls."

"I was never good at baseball, remember?" I say dryly.

He snorts. "No. You sure weren't, but what I'm trying to say is I think he's someone who will help you find your missing piece. So enjoy the ride, even if it's to an unknown destination. Until I met Martin, I didn't know I was missing something. He just fell into my life and it's been amazing. Like, I can see a rainbow instead of a bug splattered windshield."

"Stop with your mushy poetic stuff." I mock gag. "You're so in love it's sickenin'."

I say it with a smile, though. He knows I'm kidding. Because I want him to have his happiness just as much as my own.

Dan is the eternal optimist. Even when he didn't think he could find love for himself, he never completely snuffed out the idea. Every situation thrown his way from his grandfather's sudden death and a change in his own plans, to finding his calling with the ranch. He has a knack for taking all the shit that comes his way and making it smell good.

"I'm going to take him by the old property tomorrow, I think? We'll go look at that sleigh first, but before I meet his dad, I want him to know where I come from. Parents always ask the boyfriend about their own parents and I don't want to lie."

"He's not going to run, Blaze."

Running a finger around the edge of my cup, I shrug. "I hope not."

CHAPTER 17

RIVER

"I don't ever want to know, oh oh — "

"You need to stop singing along." I say, laughing so hard I might have to pull over.

Since I picked up Blaze this morning, he promptly took over the radio and let it stop at a country station. I've got nothing against country music. I do, however, need Blaze to stop singing. He's not horrible by any means, but sometimes he tries to make me laugh, hitting high notes and singing the wrong words.

Then he smiles that smile that's only for me and I have trouble concentrating on the road. So really, he's putting our lives in danger by singing.

"You wound me, River."

He flicks off the radio with a grin. "Okay, no more singin'. Tell me about this master sleigh builder."

"Right, his name is Jorge and his wife is Anna. He's a second generation Portuguese immigrant, and he's an amazing builder. His dad had a construction company when they first came to Canada. Jorge learned from him."

"Wow, so he's been doin' it a long-time then. Did you ever work with him?"

"I did. Just after my mom died, I finally left the house to get a job and Jorge's dad hired me right away. I helped with custom cabinets for a few months and his dad taught me so much."

Signalling to a side road, my truck leaves the pavement and we continue along a gravel country road. Fields, trees and livestock keep us company for the rest of the way.

"That's really cool. Do you keep in touch?"

"A little. Since Anna got sick, he's busy with the kids and his parents live with him too now. With all that and working to keep the cash coming in, he hasn't had time for social things. I try to call him every few months, just to let him know I still think of him. Which I do, but he never wants to ask for help. If I offer, he almost always declines it."

"What would he do if you just helped and didn't offer? Would he be offended?"

Mulling it over, I'm not sure what Jorge would do. He's such a proud man, and he respects what his dad built for them after coming here. But he's also ashamed for the business floundering for the same reason. He couldn't have predicted his wife getting sick and that had to take priority.

"I'm not really sure, actually."

Blaze gazes out the window as we travel in silence, and I know he's likely cooking up a way to help. If there's one thing about him I admire, it's his want to always try to make a situation better for someone. While he doesn't like to advertise he has money, I know it bothers him to just have it when someone else needs it. But even if it's a problem that can't be solved with money, Blaze is still one actively trying to find a solution.

It's honestly my favourite thing about him. Okay, that's not totally true. It's probably all those little smile lines around his eyes when he smiles big. But I love what's in his heart. He's so pure of intention it's frightening. But that's who Blaze is and I'm damn lucky he lets me see that part of him.

Slowing, I ease my truck into the yard of Jorge and his family. Both kids are playing in the yard and stop to see who's visiting. Jorge opens the door of the Quonset hut workshop before we've even stepped out of the truck.

"River!" He dusts his hands on his pants and briskly crosses the short distance from his shop to me.

"It's so good to see you, my friend." I say as we hug tightly.

"You too, River. You too. What brings you by? Can I get you anything?" He fires questions, always the host.

"No, we don't need anything, thank you. But I want you to meet someone first." Blaze offers his hand with a warm smile and Jorge shakes it with his paw-sized hand. "This is my friend Blaze. He owns the ranch with Dan."

"Pleasure to meet you, Jorge. River says many kind words about you."

"All of them deserved." I add before Jorge goes into his routine of denying everything. "We'd like to talk about the sleigh, if you still have it?"

"Yes, come to the back of the yard with me."

Blaze follows Jorge, but I turn back to where I know Abby and Arthur are politely holding back. They don't come forward unless invited usually, but I know it's okay with Jorge for me to say hello.

"Hey kiddos, long time no see. Do I get a hello?"

Abby runs up right away and I bend down to hug her. "You're getting so big! How are you two?"

Arthur, the more serious of the two, offers his hand to shake. He's never been a kid to go for hugs. "We're okay. Are you here to help daddy?"

"I hope to buy the sleigh he built. Maybe I can take you for a ride on it sometime."

Abby claps her hands. "Yes! With the big horses?"

"Exactly." I glance back to see Blaze and Jorge have disappeared around the house. "Listen, kids, I need to catch up. Stop eating all the weeds. That's why you're growing like one!"

They giggle and return to their game and I jog to the back, where I know Jorge has the sleigh. I find him and Blaze already leaning against it, deep in conversation.

"Did you make a deal already?" I ask when I finally reach ear shot.

"We're about to, I think." Blaze throws his smile my way and places his hand on my back. I wrap an arm around his waist as Jorge grins.

"It makes more sense now. Why didn't you introduce him as your boyfriend, River?"

Jorge still smiles, but I'm a little confused.

"What makes sense?"

Blaze makes an exaggerated gesture to Jorge, asking him to not say anything, and my friend smiles more.

"He'll have to tell you." He reaches out a hand to Blaze to shake. "But you've got yourself a deal. I can drop it off at the ranch next week and you can hitch up to the wagon to take now."

"Wagon?" I look to Blaze and find him smiling.

"I'll tell you on the way home. But first we have a wagon to hitch."

Jorge and Blaze get to work removing the hitch for horses on a gorgeous wooden wagon and I bring the truck around. We don't have it wired for tail lights so Jorge sets us up with long fluorescent poles and hazard cloths to keep things safe.

Once we've said our goodbyes and Blaze made the arrangements with Jorge for paying, I drive us out of the yard heading home.

"Okay, what's with the wagon?" I ask once we start down the bumpy road.

Blaze is silent for some time, but I give him space to answer.

"You said you weren't sure if he'd just accept help. We were talkin' and he said he had made the sleigh for someone who backed out of the deal. Did you know that?"

"I did."

"Anyway, I saw the wagon there, and I said, is that for sale too? He said yes, but because of the custom welding he had done to make the rails and reinforce the underside, it was a higher cost than what other wagons sold for. He hasn't been able to sell it."

"And you bought it."

"I did. It's quality work, and I didn't want him takin' a loss to unload it. He said he was thinkin' of doin' that and lowballed his offer to me." Blaze chews his lip. "So I offered him more than that and to be fair, he saw right through me." He laughs. "Jorge knew I was a horrible business man inflatin' the price and told me the original price, so we agreed on that."

"But we don't need a wagon."

"We don't. But I'm sure we can find somethin' to do with it."

The empty wagon bumps along behind us on the country road, and Blaze stares back out the window. If I didn't know better, I'd think there's something bothering him. Reaching over, I find his hand and grip it tightly in mine.

"Something on your mind? You've been... different today."

His hand squeezes mine, and he nods.

"I want to show you somethin' today. But I'm nervous about what you'll think of it."

"What is it?"

Blaze chews on his lip and runs his thumb over my knuckles. "I want to show you where I came from. Where I grew up."

"Like a house?"

"Sumthin' like that." He puffs out a breath. "I want to know just in case... in case you don't want to be around me after."

"That's nonsense. Nothing is going to make me not want to be around you."

He nods, convincing himself my words are true. "Then let's drop the wagon at the ranch first. We'll feed Mando and take my truck. Is that okay?"

"Whatever you'd like Blaze. I'm fine with that."

What I'm not fine with is how the Blaze I'm growing quite fond of is disappearing before my eyes.

After we dropped the wagon at the ranch and stopped to change trucks at Blaze's, we were once again driving out of town.

Blaze's fingers grip and re-grip the steering wheel with one hand and his other taps at his thigh. He's been eerily quiet and far removed from the happy singer of this morning.

Reaching over, I take his hand in mine, threading our fingers together with a squeeze.

"Want to talk about it?"

His eyes flick to mine and back to the road.

"I'd rather wait until we get there."

His voice is quiet, like we're whispering in church and I don't like it. My skin feels too tight and I hate the way my mind races. I'm adrift, wondering if whatever he's about to show me will be the end of us. We've only just begun and whatever is going through his mind, I hope he unloads soon.

The truck slows, and he takes us down a dusty side road for several kilometers before finally slowing again and turning into a tiny lane overgrown with grass from lack of use, but you can tell there's still tracks for tires from days long ago.

There are a lot of potholes and I'm thankful the fall rain hasn't started yet, or we'd need to use 4x4 to get out. If we could get out, that is.

One side of the lane is a mix of trees making what I imagine is a property line and the other side is an open field. There are no meadow flowers or fancy grasses. It's just a barren piece of land. The longer we drive down this path, the more confused I get.

Blaze shifts down to creep us through a bumpy patch, and that's when I notice the lake ahead of us. It's dark and spreads so far I can't see where it ends. It's probably really pretty in the spring, but right now it's cold and harsh and devoid of surrounding greenery.

When he puts the truck in the park, Blaze remains staring at the lake, hands clutching the wheel. I don't want to interrupt him, but I place my hand on his thigh to let him know I'm here.

Surveying the area around the lake, I notice a tiny trailer off in what was probably a clearing at one point. Its roof is sinking in and it hasn't been occupied for a long time. But it has the skirting around the bottom and a woodpile nearby to show someone used to use it frequently.

Blaze clears his throat, and I notice his pulse pounding at the spot on his neck.

Finally, with an inhale, he turns his sad eyes to me.

"This is where I come from, River. This is how I grew up."

"You lived here?"

Surely not in the trailer I was just looking at. But he nods and exits the truck, so I do what I'll always do with Blaze.

I follow him.

CHAPTER 18

BLAZE

Standing in front of the broken-down house-trailer I grew up in, I force a laugh as River comes up beside me.

"I guess I really am trailer trash."

River's silence makes the knot in my stomach tighten. I knew I needed to show him this before I could allow myself to keep moving forward with him. My heart had already attached itself to him and before I dove into the deep end, I wanted to make sure it had a life preserver. He could still change his mind now and the wounds wouldn't be as deep. I could survive it. But before I invested myself fully in another relationship, I had to know where he stood with this.

He's not Ted. I know that. But it's important to me for him to accept this part of my past. It's ugly, but there's no way to make it pretty. This is what I am.

"You're not trash. Not even close, so don't say that."

River takes a few steps towards the collapsing corpse of a trailer. "Is it okay for me to get closer?" He looks over his shoulder and I nod to continue.

He walks through the overgrown grass and stops short at the front door. With the toe of his boot, he nudges the wooden step there. I split my lip on it when I was seven. The step crumbles with his poke and River jumps back, eyes wide. The window remains intact which is strange, but it's not like he can peer inside. It's covered in bird shit and bugs and spider webs and whatever else nature does to abandoned buildings once people leave.

The fall peepers are singing around the lake and soon it will be too dark to see your hand in front of your face. I hated the darkness out here when I was a kid. The outhouse seemed so far away in the deep black of night. If the moon wasn't shining bright, I'd hold it until the morning.

River returns to where I've remained firmly rooted, and the knot in my gut grows so tight I can taste the bile rising in my throat. Standing in front of me, he tilts his head back slightly and his brown eyes shimmer with unshed tears.

"Tell me what made you bring me here. Why did you cause yourself so much pain to show me this?" His rough palm cups my cheek and I close my eyes, leaning into his touch.

"I want you to know what I was. What I still am. Before we go any further with us, you need to know who I am."

"I know who you are. You're kind and gentle. You're funny and sweet. And you're a man who leads by example. You're selfless, a loyal friend, an animal lover, and the best kisser I've ever had."

I allow my lips to twitch into a smile as his thumb swipes away the tear on my cheek.

"I'm also the kid who didn't go to school until he was ten because his dad needed him to work at home. The kid who still didn't have runnin' water and boiled water on a wood stove to take a bath with a bucket outside. I'm the kid whose parents were so poor and uneducated when my mom got pneumonia they tried to treat it with herbs and tea from pine trees." I sniffle and choke on my next words. "Spoiler. It didn't work."

River, to his credit, shows no shock or disgust. He listens, so I spill out my ugly past through my tears.

"I was nine when she died and I walked into town with a note to the welfare office asking for help. But my dad couldn't spell worth shit and I had to explain what happened. A funeral home eventually came to take her body away and then social workers took me." I gesture to the trailer. "I ran away and came back here. I thought my dad would want me to be with him, but he didn't. I don't know how or where he found booze, but he was an alcoholic. I didn't understand then, but I do now. He was drinking away all his pain."

Vaguely, the squeeze of River's hands on mine shifts my attention to his face. Through my teary vision, all I see is a man who really adores me. There's no judgment, only empathy, and I wiggle a hand free to run my thumb over his tears.

"When I was thirteen, I finally left here for good. A teacher at my school let me stay with her until they could find a place for me. She risked her job to do that, but she knew I was takin' showers in the school locker room every day and sleepin' in coffee shops or parks until someone found me or asked me to leave. It was only a matter of time before they forced me into foster care again, and I didn't want that."

"Why? You didn't want to find a family to care for you again?"

I shrug, my shoulders heavy. "I did, but I don't know why I kept runnin'. I think I was afraid of it all happenin' again."

"What changed?"

"I went to a Boys and Girls Club one day. The sign had big red letters and promised they excluded nobody. As you can probably tell, I was bullied a lot at school and I kept to myself. I thought maybe kids were different at the club." A genuine smile fills my face with the memory. "And they were. I met Dan there."

River brings my hand to his lips, placing a soft kiss on my knuckles. "And you made a friend. A true friend since he's still in your life."

"I don't know how we clicked, but we did. It was this instant friendship, and he was the first kid that didn't look at me funny when I spoke. This weird accent I have is just because I only had my parents to model after. I learned it and couldn't change it, even when I tried."

"I happen to like your accent. It's one of the first things I noticed about you. Right after I saw you on Joker looking like something out of The Cowboy Digest." He places a soft kiss on my lips. "Then you opened your mouth and my crush was instant."

His happy grin makes my heart lighter and eases the knot in my stomach.

"I wanted you to see this because it's important to me. It embarrassed me for a long time. My ex, Ted, when the topic of family came up, and I told him about this place, you know what he said? He said I should never let a soul know about this. It would ruin my image and nobody would want to do business with me. I'd be an outcast in the business world. After he knew about this, our relationship changed. It was like all he could see when we were together was some unwashed kid with old clothes. He made me so ashamed to talk about... my parents." Angrily, I swipe at my eyes as the tears flow. "They loved me and did what they could. If mom hadn't of got sick... life would have been a lot different, I think."

River's eyes flash with anger. "Well, Ted's fucking wrong. Look at what you overcame to get to where you are now. That's not something to be ashamed of. You should be proud. As children, we don't get to decide who our parents are or where we live. None of that was in your control. Hell, even if it was, what a shitty thing to say. Fuck, Blaze, he was an asshole to ever make you feel that way."

"That's what Dan always says, too."

"He's your best friend and you're not listening to him?"

Ducking my head, I chuckle. "I can be stubborn that way."

River brings his hands to my face with a firm grip and forces me to look at him. And when I do, I stop breathing.

"I think I know where this is coming from, Blaze. But know this. I'm dying for you to meet my dad and I'm not ashamed to bring you there." He plants a soft yet firm kiss on my lips, and I pull him into a tight hug. I gulp lungfuls of air and hold him tight. He saw this hovel of a home and knew all my intimate details and didn't want to run.

"Can we go home now? Or is there more you want to show me here?"

He snuggles under my arm, wrapping his arms around my waist and he feels perfect there. Like he was custom made, and we scripted this moment for us.

"Have you ever been fishin'?" I ask as I walk him closer to the edge of the lake. "Or even catch a frog?"

"I have, but it's been a real long time since I've done either."

"I'll take you in the spring."

A fish jumps as we stand at the lake edge and we both point to the splash, watching the rings on the water find their way to the shore. A pang of nostalgia hits me. Not everything here is sad. I used to love taking the tiny canoe out and listening to the ducks, frogs, and fish jumping. Sometimes I stayed out past dark to watch the stars as long as the moon was bright.

There was love here once. Before things got messy and complicated and it forced me to grow up far too soon. Before the path laid for me got so bumpy, I often felt sick from all the ups and downs.

Maybe one day I'll love it again and I can smooth it all out.

River locks eyes with me and his special smile wraps around me. I bet I can if River is here to help me do it.

CHAPTER 19

RIVER

Our drive home is quiet, but it's comfortable. The tension Blaze carried on our drive out to his childhood home is gone and replaced with something else I can't quite put my finger on.

I flipped back the console between us so I could sit closer to Blaze. I needed to be next to him and I think he needed that, too. Our legs pressed together and my hand on his thigh felt... different. Like something connecting us more than just our bodies touching. It ran deeper, and I felt it to my soul.

Today was unexpected, and Blaze keeps revealing all these layers to him. Like those nesting dolls when you think you've finally unwrapped the last one, another one pops up. When he purchased the wagon from Jorge that we didn't need just to help him, my heart burst and I thought I couldn't fall for this man anymore than I already have. But watching him cry and hearing how he lost his mother unnecessarily? That broke me. Knowing a cold and hungry Blaze lived in that trailer for most of his young life stirred up feelings I'm not familiar with.

I don't completely understand why he's ashamed of it, though. But it explains why he's been a little hesitant to keep our relationship moving forward. We've had a few dates since the night of the fundraiser, but nothing more than making out has happened. We had the one hot session on his couch and it's been kisses and gentle groping since.

Now I think I get it. A guy like Blaze is confident and secure on the outside. His shell stands up to everything and everyone. He doesn't let anyone in because at some point, he'll need to share where he came from and his family with you. Blaze views sex as a commitment and not something to just use as a means to an end. He can't help but to love because he's so full of it and it has nowhere to go. Sure, he has Dan and Mando, but that's not what he needs. He's choosing loneliness to protect himself from another repeat of Ted. I've never condoned violence, but I'd like to throat punch that Ted guy. What a jerk.

There's only one way to the inside of Blaze and it's not by his heart. It's through his brain. To show him he's worthy and perfect, just as he is. His past is just that. Something in the rear-view mirror. While he had a rough start with life, it makes him a better person for me. He's stronger for it. Even Ted, in some way, strengthened him. But it's my mission now to win all of him. I want to peel away that last layer he's holding back.

I want his heart, because he sure as hell has mine.

When he finally pulls into his driveway, he kills the engine and turns to me.

"Do you want to come in, or do you need to get home?"

"I don't need to go home."

His smile is shy again as he nods. "Good. Ah, then let's... go in?"

I laugh and peck a kiss on his cheek. "Yes, that's what you do when you get home, usually."

Reluctantly, I release our hands and slide over to exit from the passenger side. With house keys in hand, he meets me with a kiss in front of the truck and I wrap an arm around his waist as we walk to the front door.

Once inside, Mando meows and comes running over. Blaze scoops him up as he always does, kissing his furry face and delivering a rough ear scratch. The cat chirps his happiness in return. People say men with babies are an aphrodisiac but I'd like to motion it's men loving on their ridiculously cute fur babies that turns my crank.

Blaze places Mando back on the floor and he prances away, pleased with his daddy's love. The smile on Blaze's face over that damn cat is my undoing.

"Blaze?"

"Mmm?" He hums as he toes off his boots while I do the same.

"Did you have any plans when you invited me in?"

"Uh, not really. I just... I didn't want to be alone tonight."

His throat clicks when he swallows down his admission, and I step into him.

"I don't either. Let me... let me show you how I feel about you? Please?"

One of those charged moments passes between us again before he nods and I bury my face in his neck. He smells like our long day mixed with the citrusy cologne he only wears when we're together. His pulse slams out of control on his neck and I nip the area before soothing it with a kiss.

Searching out his skin, my hands slide under his t-shirt as he gasps.

"Your hands are freezin'."

"Sorry. Your skin is hot. You're hot." I peel off his shirt as he sways on his feet. "C'mon. Let me take care of you."

Blaze only nods and follows me along to his bathroom. His huge bathroom with all the fancy lights and controls that I've been curious about since the first time I saw it. The shower is big enough to seat a party of six, so that's where I'd like to start. There's just something about benches in showers that call out for you to use it for debauchery. That's my story and I'm sticking to it.

"Show me how to work this thing."

Blaze laughs and reaches into the shower, pressing some buttons on a panel. In seconds, short bursts of steam fill the shower and the water cascades from the overhead shower head.

"What? No mood lighting?"

"I feel like you're in a devilish mood." He presses another button, and a muted red glow swathes the entire bathroom. I wouldn't have thought the colours of lights would have any bearing on my libido, but you learn something new every day. With a devilish grin of his own, he speaks to his google home control. "Hey google, play sultry sex mix."

"Why do you have a sultry sex mix on your playlist Mr.Porter? Have you been holding out on me?"

"I've been holdin' out *for* you, I think, is the better wordin'"

With a shaky breath, I step closer to pop the button on his jeans and unzip him, pushing his jeans to the floor. He pulls my shirt over my head, smoothing his hands over my chest in silent appreciation. The playlist is indeed sultry. Saxophones seem to pair well with red lighting. Who knew?

I shuck my own pants and boxers quickly and stand in front of Blaze naked as the bathroom fills with more steam from the fancy shower. His throat bobs with a swallow as he reaches out to fondle my heavy balls. "I want to feel these slapping against me. I don't care where." Leaning in, he kisses me, soft and tender, but he vibrates with an unspoken message.

His voice is raw with desire, but his shaky touch tells me there's so much more here and I silently wish for him to say it. To know I'm safe and let me be the one to love him like he deserves.

"I'll do whatever you want, but not until I get to know every inch of you first." Trailing kisses and small licks down his chest and stomach, I sink to my knees in front of him and slide his boxers down his legs. His cock springs free, already so fucking hard he must be in pain. I can't resist a taste and I flick my tongue over his slit, basking in the low curse Blaze mutters.

"I brought you back here to spoil you. I'm not always good with words and sex can be... misunderstood sometimes. I want to take care of you and show you what you mean to me. I want to do that for you, Blaze."

Wordlessly, he nods and I pull him into the shower, which is more erotic than I imagined a shower could be. Standing him under the giant shower head, he watches me with wet eyelashes as I find his soap. It's citrusy, like his cologne, and I wonder if he buys them to complement each other. With a gentle hand, I cover his body with slippery suds and linger on the sensitive parts. My thumbs graze over his nipples and when he allows his head to drop back with pleasure, I cover his throat with kisses while his erection pokes into my stomach.

He's fucking perfection. So beautiful and pliant under my touch. My whole soul aches to join with his.

I turn him around and wash his hair from behind, taking a little longer to massage his scalp and his contented sighs are music to my ears. My cock slides over the cleft of his ass when I lean in to kiss down his back. He pushes his ass out towards me, a silent message to pay attention to it, and I give his shoulder a little bite.

The sounds of sexy saxophones, small puffs of steam, and Blaze's sighs and moans fill the bathroom. He's lost in the simple pleasure of allowing himself to feel good and I am too, but for me, this isn't all about the pleasure. It's the man in my arms. I'm on the edge of losing myself to him completely and I want him to know I'll take care of him and his heart. I'll guard it and him like the treasure they are. I'm falling in love with this beautiful, broken, gorgeous man and I don't want to stop this feeling.

Eyeing up the height of the shower bench and considering the hard tile of the shower, I whisper against his ear.

"Do you think you can stand on the bench without falling and breaking anything?"

He laughs a bit and reaches his arm around to hold me still for a deep kiss. "I can. What did you have in mind?"

I smack a wet hand on his tight ass. "I won't have to kneel on the hard tile to eat you. If you stand, I'll only have to bend a little. I want to rim you until your legs quiver and we have to stop before you pass out."

"Fuck." He rasps.

I laugh against his lips. "Eventually yes."

He steps up and braces his hands on the wall, spreading his legs and tilting his ass for access and it's a fucking vision that, if I could, I'd carve it on a statue right this second to preserve it. Thank god for his hot water on demand system because I don't want to rush this. Hell, I don't ever want to end this. I could stay here until I'm waterlogged and do this all night.

Spreading his cheeks, I groan before I say fuck the finesse and dive in. I know I said I wanted to be slow, but even I have some limits on how much edging I can handle. Having Blaze's tight ass and pink hole in my face seems to be the tipping point for me.

"River... oh fuck, River..."

Blaze writhes under my mouth, slapping at the wall. My fingers grip tightly so he can't move and my tongue works past the tight ring of muscle while my cock begs for attention. It's only when Blaze's legs tremble and my own quads scream from the position that I reluctantly pull away and help him down.

His body is flushed from arousal and most likely the steam, and I wonder if the steam makes you more sensitive. With any luck, I can test that theory tomorrow morning.

"Are you okay?" I ask and smooth the hair back from his forehead.

His eyes are glazed but clear as he presses his lips into mine. "Fantastic. And so hard. I need to come so bad." He laughs softly and when I wrap my hand around his hard cock, his moan has me torn over if I should just jack him off here or wait until I'm inside him.

"Turn this sex trap off and we can both come."

Blaze fumbles with the buttons and the room changes colours a few times before he gets the lights to go off. Ripping a towel off the rack, I pat him dry and take the time to get all the spots between the toes and under his arms. The entire time, his hooded gaze stays on me and when I look up from my place on the floor, I see my emotions mirrored on his face. This is not just sex to him.

I barely dry myself off in the haste to get to the bedroom. Blaze fucking Porter, the man I've been quietly wishing I could have for over a year, is now spread out on his bed for me. A panting mess begging for me to finish him off. I did this. He wanted me to take him apart and my hands shake with nerves as he tosses lube and a condom on the bed in my direction.

I lean down and take his mouth with a kiss that he returns with a bruising force as he pushes against my slicked up fingers.

"Stop teasin' me." He mumbles against my lips. "Gimme the D and stop makin' me beg. Cuz I'm beggin' and I hate the way I sound."

"I love hearing you beg for my cock. That's fucking hot. But I won't ever make you beg. For anything."

I'm relieved I don't fuck up the condom the first time, because he's not the only one out of practice and I press against his softened hole. I'm not an overly endowed guy. I've got enough of a dick I know how to use it and a talented mouth to go with it. Nobody has ever complained. But right now, the tightness of Blaze makes me feel like I'm a giant.

"You good?" I whisper when he gasps as my balls graze his ass.

"Impossibly good. More than good."

Sitting back on my knees, I hold his legs out and stare down at my cock sliding in and out of his ass before watching the expressions cross his face. Bliss. That's what I settle on because it's what I feel too.

"I'm not made of glass. Make me feel it, Riv. Balls slappin', remember?"

I snort a laugh before angling my hips to find the sweet spot and when his mouth drops open in an O, I know I found it. Then I rail him just like he asked me to.

"Ohmygod... fuck, fuck, gonna come... "

Blaze's hand moves on his cock as I dive again and again into him, spurred on by his sexy moans and pleas to not stop.

"I'm right behind you, baby. Paint your chest with it."

Blaze throws his head into the pillow with a shout loud enough to rattle the pictures, but it takes me over the edge with him. I groan, filling the condom and slowing my thrusts until I'm sure we can't possibly have any more cum left in us. Easing out, I lay next to him, brushing the hair from his forehead.

"Are you okay?" I place a kiss on his temple before rolling over to deal with the condom. "I'll be right back."

I toss the condom in the garbage and return with a warm wet cloth to clean him up with. He's still panting and my chest puffs with pride that I wrecked him so well he can barely breathe. Score one for the shorter guy with an average sized dick. Tossing the cloth near his hamper, I wait for him to open his eyes so we can talk.

It's been a very emotional day. More for him, but I had a lot to deal with, too. We're both spent physically and I don't want to assume anything.

"Nobody has ever made me feel like that, Riv. Nobody." He turns his head on the pillow and his soft gaze lands on my lips. I reach forward and kiss him.

"Feel like what?"

"Like I'm the most cherished person on the planet and you didn't want to just have sex. You wanted somethin' more, didn't you? Am I wrong thinkin' there was a lot more goin' on tonight?"

His eyes shine with hope and internally, I kick this Ted guy's ass. Again.

"There's a lot more going on. You're right. I... I was hoping you could tell how much I... ," It's too soon for me to say that, I think. Or should I? Because if I'm honest, I think I loved him the moment he stabbed me with that vaccine. "I hope you could feel how much I want to write that book with you."

His eyebrows furrow with confusion.

"After our date and we fooled around on your couch, you said you wanted to start a new chapter." His eyes widen and I lean over to kiss him again. "I don't want a chapter, Blaze. I want the whole fucking book."

CHAPTER 20

BLAZE

S watting at whatever is tickling my nose, I crack an eye open to find Mando sitting next to my head and reaching a paw out to tap my nose.

"You really can't just let me sleep in, can you?"

With a chirp he jumps down, running out of the room to the kitchen now that I'm awake. Damn cats and their food clocks.

Turning my head, River's back faces me and he's thrown off most of the covers. My gaze travels from his shoulders down his spine to the cleft of his ass peeking out from under the duvet. My heart races, recalling what we did last night and the words we said. Especially how he didn't care about my family history. That, more than anything, sticks to my brain.

I can never erase the look on Ted's face when I shared a picture of the trailer and my story. If I had brought him here in person, he'd likely have run away or thrown up. It might have saved me a lot of heartache if I had. Why I allowed him to get to me so much I don't really know, but it did. It's been a hell of a battle convincing my head that my past doesn't define me.

River stirs and the duvet slips lower, showing off more of his ass, and I stifle a moan. I want to stay in bed all day with him. Just as I reach over to slide the blanket down further, a loud meow sounds from the kitchen.

"Damn cock blockin' cat." I mutter and River stirs again. This time rolling over and blinking sleepy eyes my way.

Holy fucking hot cakes. He's even sexier than I imagined with sleep mussed hair and pillow lines on his cheek.

"You should go feed Mando and come back here for a while."

He moves the covers, revealing his semi hard cock waking up with him.

I bend forward and kiss his temple. "I like that plan. Don't start without me."

"Wouldn't dream of it." He drawls.

Bare-assed, I wander to the kitchen where Mando waits for his breakfast at his dish with a put-out look on his face.

"Your breakfast is only late by twenty minutes. Don't act like you've never been fed."

The kibble plinks into his bowl and he chirps away as he waits for me to slop a spoonful of wet food on top. He always eats that first and if I forget to give it to him, he lets me know. Loudly.

As I place the food back in the fridge, my phone buzzes on the counter. I shouldn't look and just go back to the sexy man waiting in my bed, but old habits die hard and I look, anyway.

I wish I hadn't.

Ted's name is there and I can only read the first few lines of the text message.

Ted: I know you hate me but...

With a deep breath, I let my curiosity continue to win and open the message.

It's long. As I read through it, two more come through from him.

The more I read, the more confused I get. But there's also anger. Because I thought this was over and buried. He was in the past and the agreement was to never contact me again. And yet... I think I need to accept this request. Not for him, but for me.

"Hey, is everything okay?"

River appears, just as naked as I am, with a worried and lopsided grin. I must have been gone longer than I thought.

"You didn't come back, so I thought I'd check on you."

Tossing the phone on the counter, I step into him, wrapping him in my arms. Fuck, he feels so good like this. So perfect and kind. So non judgemental and safe.

"I'm sorry. My phone went off and for some reason, I had to check it."

"What happened? You sound tense."

Puffing out a breath, I bury my face in his shoulder and his arms instantly pull me closer. His lips next to my ear eases the tension and I'm grateful.

"Whatever it is, Blaze, I'm here and I'll help you through it. Don't think you're alone, 'kay?"

Pulling away, I gaze into his warm eyes and I know he's telling me the truth. Inherently, I trust him and believe him.

"Do you think you'd be able to come to Rosevale with me for a few days next week?"

"Um, I'd have to ask for the time off and as long as I could swing it, I would. I don't get paid until next Friday, but I can —"

I cut him off with a finger over his lips. "I know the boss, remember? We'll work out the cover for both of us and you're my guest. I don't want you to pay."

He's quiet a moment and I can tell he's thinking. Maybe too hard, but I need him there with me if I have to face that man again. I don't know what I'll do on my own.

"I don't want it to look like I'm taking advantage of either you or Dan. I don't want the others to think I get special treatment."

"Ah, I see. Well, Riv, that's somethin' that comes with datin' a guy like me. I treat you special because you are. I can't help it, I'm your boss too. But I'd never want to make it uncomfortable for you. I haven't yet have I?"

He bites his lip as his eyes search my face, reading the sincerity there.

"No, you haven't. I just... I don't want you to think I'm taking advantage. I'm not in this for an all expense trip to Rosevale or whatever is in your wallet."

"I know, Riv. You're not like the others." I snort. "Actually, you might like what's in my wallet. I still have a condom in there from a few weeks ago."

That makes him smile, and he presses his lips against mine so soft and sweet I sigh against him.

"Okay, I'll go. What's it about?"

"I just got a text from Ted and he wants to speak to me in person."

River sets his jaw and a thrill runs through me with his instant protection mode.

"Well, just so you know, I can't be held responsible for anything I might do or say in his presence."

Laughing, I wrap my arm around his waist and pull him back to me, kissing his frown off his face.

"You can read the message. Normally I would've just said fuck you, but I think I need to speak to him. For my purpose and not his."

River hesitates when I hold my phone to him with the message open. "I trust you Blaze. I don't need to read it."

"I know, but tell me if there's somethin' there that sounds like I should ignore it."

River's brow scrunches as he reads and absently rubs a hand over his stomach. "It sounds like he's having a crisis and wants to make amends with you. That's how it reads to me."

"Yeah, I got the same vibe. He really did a number on me and while hate is a strong word, I can't let anyone suffer. But not at my expense either. Not anymore."

"I know. You're one of the softest and kindest people I know. Even if he is an ex, make sure he's okay. You'd feel horrible if you didn't." As much as I tried to forget the whole thing with Ted. River is right. There's something needy in his phrasing, causing me to want to honour his request. Even if I wish we'd never met most days.

River kisses down my throat, bringing me back to present thoughts and it's now I remember we're still buck naked in my kitchen on a Sunday morning. The morning sun has already spread its warmth through the window and Mando spreads across its path like he does every sunny morning.

It's this that I longed for back in Dan's kitchen and, honestly, my whole life. I'd miss it too if River was suddenly gone. Maybe a little too much.

We may have only just started along the path of falling for each other, but I don't want to stop.

River makes me feel things I've only ever dreamed about. He makes me believe I'm worthy of love and he makes me want to stop watching from the sidelines.

As River's lips move across my skin, and his hands trail down to my ass, I know even with us moving faster than I was ready for, it's right. This is what I've been searching for. All of it.

"Let's take this back to the bedroom, Riv. This body can't handle granite countertops and porcelain tile floors right now."

His eyes twinkle, and he wiggles his eyebrows. "You could always start up your love shower again. We could get clean and dirty at the same time."

I bark out a laugh.

"You're gonna be addicted to that, aren't you?"

"Only if you're in it with me."

He turns and saunters his way back towards the bathroom, lily-white ass swaying as he goes and even though I need to return to Rosevale and face some unaddressed feelings, I can do anything with River with me.

"All you need to do is the regular maintenance for the other horses with them. I've got lots of time to get them used to the sleigh when

I come back." I'm walking through the draft horse barn with Alec so he can cover things while I go back to the city. He nods and listens, but I can tell he's distracted.

"Spill it. Is this about our sunrise coffees? Did I let you down or somethin'?"

"What? No! I'm fine. Sorry, just distracted. How long will you be gone for?"

Alec removes his hat and scratches his head. The dark circles around his eyes concern me.

"Hey, it's not my business, but is everythin' okay with you and your friend?"

His expression immediately shutters and his lips press tight. "Yep."

Alec pulls a crumpled bag of candy from his pocket and reaches inside. He opens his hand with a smile at the bubble gum pieces, small plastic horse and wrapped fizz candies.

"Want something?"

I pluck the fizz candy out of his hand as he hides the horse in his pocket with a small smile.

"Do you think Colby knew there was a horse in that bag for you?"

"It's a *surprise* bag, Blaze. Nobody knows until you open it."

He's so serious and I was only joking, but he pops the gum in his mouth and I recognize the look he's trying to hide. A lost soul searching for a safe landing. And if he's in love with a straight friend, well, that's a whole other ball game. But I can help with one at least.

"You know, I didn't come from money. I grew up very poor. Not far from here, actually." I lean against the stall of my favourite

Percheron, Thunder. "I was lucky enough to meet Dan and his family when I was young and they gave me what I never had. A home I felt safe in. I may be out of line here, but I can tell when there's somethin' not right. And you, friend, are a salmon swimmin' upstream right now."

"What the actual fuck does that mean?"

Chuckling, I gesture for him to follow me to the ranch main yard.

"Look around here, Alec. This is your safe place. Every single one of us here will go to bat for you. We'll bail you out, stand up for you, beside you, or in front of you. Don't fight against the allies you have here. If you need an ear, there's lots around. Look how you became friends with Dante so quickly. Talk to him if you feel more comfortable. But I promise you," I place a hand on his shoulder with a squeeze. "We're all here for each other in this mixed up group of crazy love. So take it. You know we're all here for you."

He says nothing and I don't expect him to just yet. He has to accept it in his own time and terms.

"I'll make sure the drafts are taken care of and you be sure to enjoy the time away with River."

"I'd enjoy it more if it was a trip of pleasure and not business."

"Oh? I thought you were done with business?"

"Well, it's more like unresolved personal business. I asked River to come because I know I need him with me."

He considers this before squeezing my shoulder in return. "Good luck, and you two are good together. Sort it out and I'll be here."

Alec walks off to his little private cottage at the end of the yard, pulling out more candy from his pockets as he goes. I hate seeing anyone sad like he is.

Looking up at the main house, my eyes land on River exiting Dan's place and my world tilts a little when that special grin gets thrown my way.

"It's all set with Dan, and Dante is good with the extra bits. I'm all yours for three days."

"What if I want you longer?"

"I'm open for negotiation." He winks and trots backwards to his truck, out of my reach for a kiss. "I'm heading right home to pack. Then a quick stop at Dad's before I see you at your place. I won't be late."

He blows me a kiss, and I catch it like some lovesick fool and watch him drive away.

Cackling laughter from the porch has me spin around to my best friend.

"Busted. You're so far gone, there's no coming back now. You should see your goofy face."

He laughs some more, so I do what best friends do. I give him the finger.

Of course, there's no coming back now. Why would I want to return to the dull grey life of insecurities I had before?

Chapter 21

River

W ow.

For my first flight, this is a seriously tricked out plane. Excuse me, jet.

Along with the pilot and copilot, it has a flight attendant on board with the two of us. There are no rows of seats like you'd see in a normal plane, which I'm only familiar with from movies. The copilot carries our bags on for us and secures them in a little area next to the leather sofa.

"There's a sofa and reclining chairs in here, Blaze. You couldn't just fly like normal people and pay for first-class seats?"

"I could. But I hate waitin' for planes and bein' at their mercy when they're late or have staff issues or any other number of reasons to make a plane late." He takes my hand and pulls me over to the sofa. "And no first-class seat will let me be this close to you."

My hand grips his thigh a little harder than I should, and he narrows his eyes.

"Why are you nervous? Have you not flown before?"

With a breath, I shake my head. "Nope. This is quite the initiation, though. Am I allowed to open my bag in here?"

Blaze notices the constant fidgeting and squeezes my hand. "After we take off, you can."

"Salut Blaze! So nice to see you again."

The pilot, a striking older man with the beginnings of grey hair, boards the plane. His French accent is not quite lyrical like I'd expect, again from watching movies, and his dancing blue eyes land on me as he shakes Blaze's hand.

"And c'est qui ça? Blaze, is this your amour?"

I stand to shake his hand and say hello because it's the polite thing and Blaze's hand on my back takes some nerves away.

"Oui, Charles. This is River, *mon chum*."

"Welcome to my jet, River. It is my pleasure to have you and please, how do you say, *ne laisse pas celle-ci passer*."

I look towards Blaze, and he kisses me on the cheek. "I don't intend to, Charles. *Il a mon coer*."

"Ah, bon. I am happy for you, mon amie. Let's get dis bird in the air then, yes?"

Charles and the crew resume preparing us for flight and Blaze settles us back on the sofa, showing me where the seatbelts are.

"I didn't know you could speak French."

Blaze chuckles and holds my hand in his. "I wouldn't call it French. It's like a combo of French and English. Charles grew up in a small rural town much like Bloomburg, but it had a large population of French speakin' people. I met him at a bar one night and he was tryin', just like me, to hide how he talked. We hit it off and I know a few phrases and a few words here and there. I've picked up some from him, mostly."

Charles' voice comes over the speakers that we're heading towards the runway for takeoff and should be in the air shortly. My hand tightens on Blaze's.

"He's an excellent pilot. I've lost track of how many flights he's taken me on now. How come you've never flown before?"

The plane inches slowly forward, bumpy but nothing strange.

"As a kid, we didn't do vacations like that. Our family lived close by and we didn't have a lot of money, so it was never an option to fly anywhere."

"And what about once you were older and had your own life?"

His thumb strokes the back of my hand in a soothing back and forth.

"I, uh, never needed or wanted to go anywhere, I guess. I never wanted to be too far from dad just in case."

The plane's engines gear up and whine louder and suddenly we're speeding down the runway.

"What did you say to each other in French, anyway?" I ask, hoping to get my mind off the fact I'm about to be hurtling through the air in a giant metal tube.

Blaze turns my chin to have me look at him and the tenderness there makes me almost forget we're about to be flying.

"He told you to not let this one go." He drops a kiss on my forehead. "And I told him you have my heart."

The plane lifts off the ground at that moment and I have to wonder if Blaze timed those words to be delivered when my stomach swooped over the sensation of take off. But his hand cupping my head, pulling me to his lips as he whispers those words again confirms the swoop isn't from taking off.

I have his heart.

My answer to that is to kiss him back with all I have until I have to pull away with a wince.

"You didn't warn me about the ear thing." I laugh. He reaches into a pocket on the side of the sofa and holds out a stick of gum.

"This will help you."

"Big Red? They still make this stuff?" He laughs again, and it's a sound I want to hear forever. "They do somewhere. Colby got it for me. I love this stuff."

His eyes warm again as I chew on a stick of the cinnamon gum. "Well, you're officially flyin' now. Are you okay?"

"If you kiss me like that every time I'm nervous, a guy might get used to it."

"I'll kiss you like that anytime you want me to."

And just like that, I'm wondering how my life reached a point that I'm falling in love with a billionaire rancher twenty thousand feet above ground.

I may have underestimated how much wealth a billionaire has.

First the private jet. Then a hired town car and now we're entering the most opulent building I've ever set foot in and I feel like a fish in a bowl with my Walmart jeans and faded t-shirt.

Blaze grips my hand and guides me through the lobby after greeting the doorman with a hug.

"Is this a private elevator?"

"Yeah, straight to the penthouse. That's my place."

Of course it is. Mark another first time on my list and we've barely been away from home for five hours.

When the elevator opens to a warm and welcoming lobby, the nerves melt away a little. There's even a picture of the ranch hanging over a table right outside the elevator.

After opening the door, he motions for me to enter and my jaw hits the floor.

Blaze takes my bag from me, setting it next to us, and he steps in front of me.

"Darlin', look at me."

Snapping my jaw closed, I notice his furrowed brow and smooth it with a finger.

"Riv, this is what I left and I don't want it back, okay? It's not who I am, and I want you to enjoy yourself a little while you're here."

"It's really fancy. I just feel a little out of place."

He kisses my nose. "If it helps, I understand how you feel. I know what you're thinkin' because I remember how it all was for me the first time. We're all still people, and it's what's inside that matters most."

"I don't want to embarrass you." The truth tumbles from my mouth, surprising even me. I'm comfortable with him on the ranch because it's my space. But here with the flash and bright lights and my discount runners, I feel... maybe a little like second place.

"No, darlin', no. You could never. But if you want to hide out here for the next few days, we —"

"No, Blaze. I came here because you need me and you asked me to. I'll get over it. I just don't want to make things uncomfortable for you at all."

"The only thing that would make me uncomfortable is if you left."

And fuck if that statement doesn't hit me a little left of center. First the swoopy thing on the plane and now this. I wasn't expecting this to be an emotional weekend.

"You're stuck with me." I peck his lips quickly. "Just like gum on your shoe. Good luck trying to get rid of me."

He smiles genuinely and takes my hand. "Let me give you a quick tour. We'll change and I'm taking you to meet Heather."

"The woman you text every morning?" I ask as he tugs me into the master bedroom.

"Yep, that's the one."

His fingers creep into the waistband of my jeans and his grin grows wicked as he brings me closer to the picture window. A king size bed sits in the middle of the room and I'd much rather go there and get lost in him for a few hours instead of admiring his view.

Hot kisses on my neck and the tickle of his scruff run a shiver through me and I sag into his arms with a breathy sigh.

"We won't be going anywhere if you keep that up."

His lips curve against my skin as he chuckles.

"Heather would know exactly why we cancelled if I didn't show up. And I can't let her down." He squeezes me again before turning me to face him again.

The wicked grin has vanished and instead I'm left peering into the blue eyes of the man who is still stuck a little on this past life and wants me to accept this other part of him I don't know.

How could I not?

"You sure you're okay being here?"

"I'll be fine." Kissing the back of his hand, I know even if I wasn't, I'd do my best to pretend just so he'd be more at ease with it all.

"What about you though, Blaze? You have to see this guy again after how many years?"

He turns away from me and opens the closet door. "Three. Three years since I overheard him on the phone with his side piece sayin' he was only with me for the money and once he stole more money from me, he'd be set."

His shoulders sag as he pulls out dress clothes from the closet and hangs two button up shirts on the edge of the door. I clench my fists thinking about this clown who broke Blaze into little pieces.

Stepping closer, I place a hand on his back. He shakes his head with his jaw firmly set.

"I'm mostly over it. It just sometimes hurts to remember I let someone in and he abused my trust in such an epic fashion."

He swallows and pulls more clothes out of the closet and I notice he has two sets of clothes on the go.

"I didn't press charges when I found out he stole from me. I should have."

"Why didn't you?"

He holds up a tie for me and I nod in approval, so he sets it on the bed and returns to the closet.

"Because it wasn't worth it. Sure, he took my money, but in the end, what did that do to me? I have lots. Hell, I didn't even notice it was missing. Money is just money. Runnin' him through court that he wouldn't be able to pay for seemed like a bad idea." He pauses, eyes cast to the floor with a sigh. "What he took from me is something I could never get back, anyway. So the deal was he left and to never contact me again."

"But he has. That's why we're here."

Blaze motions for me to lift my arms, and he peels my t-shirt off. Silently, I watch as he removes the lavender dress shirt from the hanger and holds it up for me. I follow his lead and slide my arms through the holes.

He hums in appreciation as he buttons the shirt for me. It fits perfectly.

"Yeah, he has but... I know he deceived me once, but this feels like maybe he just wants to bury things to move on with life." He places the tie around my neck and ties it with deft fingers. "And I can't ignore that, no matter what he did. We all need to move on from things."

I know his words are true. It's just who Blaze is. I should be a little more on edge knowing I'm off to meet an ex-boyfriend who was horrible to Blaze, but I'm not. Because Blaze, I think needs this closure too. The final healing of a scar that's bigger than he lets anyone think.

"This colour is amazin' on you, Riv."

"Why do you have clothes here for me, anyway?"

Not that I'm complaining. I've never worn anything that fits this good.

"I assumed you didn't have a suit, so I sent your measurements to Heather and told her to have something here for you."

"And how do you know my measurements?" I ask as he finishes tying the tie.

He tugs on it, making me lose my balance and crash my hands into his hard chest. "Easy. I checked the tags on your clothes when you were in the shower." His smile doesn't quite reach his eyes and I feel like this whole trip will have me teetering on the edge of big emotions, finally saying them all out loud.

"I like seein' your clothes on my floor, ya know."

"Then how come you're getting me dressed?" I rasp, wishing again we could be lost in that bed together, and not stuck at a dinner table in a suit.

With a deep sigh, he releases the tie and I watch as he strips out of his clothes.

"Heather. I miss her and while she'd understand if I didn't rush off to her right away. I'd like her to know what's goin' on and get her opinion. She was there, and she knew how it all went down. Plus, I want her to meet you." He flashes his handsome smile my way.

In a moment of weakness, I ask what's been on my mind since he read that text in his kitchen.

"What exactly do you want your life to look like, Blaze? Coming here at Ted's request has raised a lot of issues for you. I know you left this behind, but what is it you want?"

He sits on the bed, and I stand in front of him. Wrapping his arms around my waist, he rests his head against my stomach.

"Simple. People I trust. My horse. My cat. Laughter." His arms squeeze tighter. "You."

The last bit is a whisper and I don't trust my voice to say anything because he's already declared so much today my head is spinning. Instead, I take his face in my hands and kiss him until he's breathless.

Then I hold him a little longer and hope he knows I want all that too.

CHAPTER 22

BLAZE

Heather needs to change jobs and become a personal shopper.

River looks hot as fuck in the fitted black suit with lavender shirt and matching tie. For something off the rack it's like a glove and I haven't missed the appreciative looks cast his way tonight either. We haven't even arrived at the restaurant yet and we've not been away from the ranch for twenty-four hours, but I've told him he has my heart and I want him in my life.

I might as well go ring shopping at the rate I'm speeding down the love highway.

That whole slow and steady thing went out the window a few days ago and I'm actually okay with it. As long as I can get through this meeting with Ted, it will be smooth sailing. I've come to realize with River's help, I'd never allowed myself any closure on that mess. I pushed it all to the back of the closet of my mind and left it there, hoping to forget about it. Ted's text made me open the door on it again, but this time for a helpful reason. I need to settle the unrest he left me with or I'll never be able to move on fully.

And River deserves all of me.

A palm smoothes up my thigh in the back of the limo and I turn to find River with a deeply furrowed brow.

"Where did you go just now?"

Dropping my head back onto the supple leather seat back I huff a breath. "Everywhere. Nowhere. Just crazy things that have happened the last few days and I've dragged you along with me."

"I wouldn't be here if I didn't want to be Blaze."

Turning my head, I find the warm eyes that always go straight to my heart. The crinkles at the edges are softer today since the smile isn't quite there. But he doesn't need his smile right now for me to believe his words. River is always a man of his word.

"I didn't expect for you to meet both ends of my world so fast, but here we are. From trailer trash poverty kid to billionaire in a penthouse and fancy suits. Eating dinner at a restaurant that probably cancelled someone's reservation for mine and dressin' you like some kind of Pretty Woman wanna be to make you fit in."

And with horror, I touch my palm to his kind face. "I hope you don't think that's what I'm doin', River. I knew you'd be uncomfortable if you stood out at the places we might go to. But when tonight is done, dress in your jeans and boots. I want you to be you."

"Blaze, I'm me, no matter what I'm wearing. I take no offense. I'm not stupid, there are dress codes and things in this life. I appreciate your thoughtfulness caring about me that way." He leans in and I meet him halfway to take a kiss, even if that's not what he was leaning closer for. "I'm here for you. Don't forget that part. That includes me wearing whatever you need me to."

His lips barely brush over mine. "You're so fucking sexy in this suit, though. I don't know what I like better. Suit Blaze or jeans and cowboy boots, Blaze."

The limo comes to a stop and we've arrived at the restaurant to meet Heather. Other than introducing Heather to River, there's nothing left in this city for me. The last few days have made it clear. Everything I want is sitting right beside me.

"Thank you. You bein' here makes this easier, you know. I appreciate it more than I can really say."

The driver opens the door and the cool breeze of evening floods in. I step out my side, buttoning my jacket against the early winter chill. River slides across the seat and I hold my hand out for him, like any gentleman would. When he takes it and his calloused palm slides into mine, my slamming heart leaps. Our eyes meet and that special smile only for me appears.

Threading my fingers through his, I lead him to the high end restaurant where a doorman welcomes us to the Vin and Vache. Not a terribly classy name, but you'll never find a better slice of beef or glass of wine. And their crème brûlée is to die for.

"Blaze!"

The sound of Heather's voice, pitched with excitement, carries over the muted conversations of diners like she just rang the bell at the New York Stock Exchange. Jumping from her chair, she throws her arms around me with strength I wasn't ready for.

"Heather, don't break me." I wheeze.

"Holy heck, I've missed you." Her eyes shine with happy tears and I blink back my own. Talking every day through text keeps us in touch, but nothing can substitute her hugs. Nothing.

"You must be River." She extends a hand to him, but as he reaches for it, she pulls him into a hug, too. "Sorry, I'm a hugger. Blaze told me you'd be okay with it, though. I'm just so excited to meet you."

River's smiling eyes meet mine before returning to Heather. "Did he now?" He ushers her back to her chair, and she grins up at him as he pulls it out for her. "If he's sharing secrets about me it's only fair for you to dish some back isn't it?"

"Hey now. I don't need you two gettin' on that well. I have a reputation at stake."

Heather smiles when River cuts in and pulls the chair next to her out for me. He leans next to my ear as he pushes in my chair. "She's wonderful, Blaze. Enjoy yourself and catch up, my love."

The words roll off his tongue, and it wasn't a mistake. He meant to say that and when he settles across from me with his easy smile and the confidence of a man who's not comfortable in his surroundings but comfortable enough to make me feel safe; I know I've found what I've been searching for. Even when I didn't know what it was. Or in this case, who it was.

Fuck this stupid dinner. He fills everything I didn't know was empty. Returning to the ranch was only the first step of my journey. Finding him was the next. River brings order to the chaos of my self-doubting brain and he adds a spoonful of sugar to my once bitter heart. He really is what I've needed all along. Someone to soften my hard edges and show me there's more to me than what I see in the mirror.

Fuck.

I just realized I'm ass over apple cart in love while the server recites the night's special of sirloin oscar with a loaded baked potato.

Heather nudges me. "You okay?"

"Never been better."

"Well, they've asked you what you'd like to drink and the server is waiting for you to stop staring at the man across the table from you."

"Right. Sorry. A whiskey sour please."

Heather cocks her head with a knowing grin. "How about we just get through the unpleasant topic first, then catch up over one of my favourite meals?"

"That sounds like a plan. You can just give me your number and text me anything you think I should know about Blaze after." River winks and Heather motions for his phone.

"I'll put my number in for you right now."

"Would you two stop? Honestly. I have no secrets."

"Did you know he has a favourite mug to drink out of when he doesn't feel well? He's literally a snarling bear until he gets tea in that mug."

"No! See, this is good to know."

River smiles my way with a wink and I can only shake my head at these two.

Heather giggles, pushing the phone back to River and he immediately texts her. I roll my eyes as they carry on like old friends. I knew they'd get along. I just didn't think it would mean so much to me to see them do it so quickly.

When the server returns for our order, I ask River if he minds if I pick something for him.

"As long as we can do that thing and pick off each other's plate if I don't like it."

"I promise you'll like it."

With a refreshed cocktail and now only waiting for our meal, I let Heather know exactly what's up and show her the message from Ted.

"I agree. It's not like him, but do you trust him? Maybe he didn't even write it?"

"I had thought about that. But there's really nothin' to gain for him."

Heather chews her lip in thought and passes the phone back to me.

"If this is some stunt, and he tries to hurt you again, I won't be happy."

River snorts. "Heather, it's why I'm here. I won't let that happen." He pins me with a gaze that is soft and determined all at once. And when he reaches across the table to hold my hand, I have to swallow back the tidal wave of emotion. "Blaze needs to do this for him, and I'll be there to help him if he needs it."

He's speaking to both of us, but that's all for me. And I hear him loud and clear.

Heather clears her throat and excuses herself to the restroom, patting my shoulder on the way by.

"I'm sorry I brought you to dinner right away. I just really wanted you to meet Heather, but I think I'm overwhelmed right now with all of this." I chuckle to myself. "This must be how you feel when you go off and whittle. I should have brought my stuff."

River brushes his lips over my knuckles. "When I said I'd be there for you, I meant it in every way. And I brought my knife and a few blocks. You can use mine. I'll give you another lesson if you want."

"You're so good to me." I breathe.

"It's easy. You're the best person I know. But can I request we don't draw out dinner? I want to be alone with you. I love Heather. She's great, but I want... things."

Nodding, I squeeze his hand back.

"Me too."

Heather isn't a best friend for nothing.

She knew I was on edge and didn't want to be out at dinner. While we took time to enjoy our meal and time together, there was no lingering over dessert and coffee like we normally would. She ordered dessert to go and said she forgot her daughter had a play practice in the morning she didn't want to be late for. After we said goodbye, River and I did the same thing and took the limo back to the penthouse.

The ride was silent, but his strong presence filled the space more than words could. The way he held my hand, made eye contact, and kissed my neck. The steady pressure of his thigh against mine. He was there for me and waiting.

And I was hanging by a thread. Every emotion and goddamn feeling under the sun was threatening to bubble over like an unwatched pot. So many things about me were boiling to the surface, and it was both a relief and a dread.

When the door of the penthouse clicks closed, I turn the deadbolt and immediately find River's strong arms around me. Clutching onto him, I bury my face in his neck.

And I fall apart.

CHAPTER 23

RIVER

Blaze was heading into the uncharted waters of self-discovery.

I know, because I'd been there myself. Throughout dinner, he tried to be present in the conversations with Heather, but both Heather and I noticed he was somewhere else. His usual animated, upbeat self was missing. When he repeatedly reached over the table to take my hand, he trembled. Blaze needs an anchor before he can address all the misplaced feelings of self-doubt and guilt. All the best friends, horses and simple country life in the world wouldn't be enough for him to make peace with what he held inside.

Ever since he showed me Ted's message, I knew this was coming. Nobody would willingly travel to speak in person to someone who had done them as wrong as Ted. Not unless there was an underlying issue they never dealt with before on their own. Or, as my intuition screams, Ted wants something, and he's hoping Blaze is easy prey again.

But I kept that to myself. He's got enough to deal with and doesn't need to add that to his plate, too.

Blaze said he returned to the ranch to seek peace and a simple life. He wanted to find what was missing. While I want to believe it's me, I'm only part of the equation.

His gentle sobs against me break my heart. When he finally settles, I guide him to the sofa and wipe off his tears. I'd sell my soul for him to never be this upset again, but it's a process he has to work through.

"You want to talk to me about it?"

He tucks under my arm and leans his head on my shoulder with a sigh.

"Sometime between readin' that text and sittin' in that restaurant, I think I had a midlife epiphany." He laughs softly as he sniffs and I pull him closer.

"I bet you did."

"I never wanted to be this kind of weak person. I don't want to cry on people's shoulders."

"Crying isn't weak. Neither are emotions, Blaze. Sharing them is courage and a sign of strength."

"Not in this world." He pulls away to look up at me. "The business world is harsh. Showin' emotion opens you to manipulation and Ted was... ,"

He trails off and settles back against me. "Ted was one of those people. Usin' me for anythin' to benefit him. I was so angry and hurt by his betrayal I've quietly hated him since. Hate, Riv. Not a mild dislike. It was like a rotten apple I refused to discard from the fruit bowl and it was spreading to the rest of me."

"That sounds awful. Is that what made you sell and leave here?"

"I think so. Everythin' I wanted was no longer bringin' me happiness. Maybe it never really did, since I ran away from the past to create this whole life I thought would solve all my problems." He walks to the windows and gazes out into the night. "I thought I was empty because I was missin' somethin'. And while it's true, that's not the whole story. I never let him explain, you know. He never once even asked to."

I'm not surprised. People like Ted tend not to explain themselves. They just move on to the next target because it's only ever about them. I'll keep that to myself, though.

"I threw anythin' I could find of his into a bag and left it down at the front desk with instructions to never let him in here. He never tried to contact me either. Which really hurt. Sure, he was cheatin' on me, but to not even try to beg or tell me it's nothin' to do with me or any of that garbage people say to lessen the hurt? That was hard to take."

He loosens his tie and, in the low glow of the moonlight through the window, he fists his hands into his hair.

"This whole time I've been thinkin' I wasn't worth even an insincere apology. I was garbage and not worthy of any happiness. I vowed I'd never let anyone get close to me like that again. Ever. Because I never wanted to feel like that again when they left. In my haste to put it behind me, I painted every man with the same brush to create distance."

He turns from the window and I want to rush him, take him in my arms and tell him he's worth everything. More than everything.

"Then I met you." He continues. "I watched you laugh on your horse that day and when you just took off on Sly like you were leavin' all your troubles behind, I envied your freedom." He takes a step closer to me. "And I watched you whittlin' off by yourself for months and you seemed so content, so happy with what you were doin'. Not just with the wood, but as you. You were this livin', breathin' mystery man who set me at ease even halfway across a field. I was too scared to get close to you, because what if I liked you?"

"But you did. Finally. That's courage, Blaze."

"Because by then that rotten apple had spread, River. I wanted what my friends had. I wanted to trust you. All the guys on the ranch respect you, and I finally allowed myself to accept it as a sign for me to just... test the waters. When you asked to teach me to whittle, I was so damn nervous. I wanted so badly to know you, but I was so fuckin' scared I'd get to know you and you'd not like the rest of me."

"If it makes you feel better, so was I. I couldn't believe a man like you would be interested at all. I wasn't even sure you'd say yes, but I asked because I already knew I'd regret it if I didn't."

What makes those special moments between two lovers seem so dreamlike? Perched on the edge of reality and fantasy? Because the two of us shared them before we even kissed and it's impossible to ignore. This invisible string pulls me over to him and I settle my hands on his hips.

"You're a good man, Blaze. Do you know why you're here to see Ted after all this time? Have you finally worked that out?"

"I need to hear what he has to say so I can kick that apple out for good. It's probably not the best thing to do, but I need it so I can move on and love someone again. The way they deserve to be loved, fully and with no reservations from me. Even if the answer is Ted telling me I was a horrible person to him first and that's why he did what he did, I have to hear it."

"It's the strongest thing you can do, Blaze. You need to say something too. Both of you have to put it out there so you can move on. The hole in your life isn't just something that's missing. It's something that needs to be repaired. Ted, in a weird way, is giving you what you need to do that. Closure is such a twisted up thing."

He rests his forehead against mine with a sigh.

"There's somethin' else, Riv."

"I'm listening. You know that."

"I love you." His palm cups my cheek and his lips slide across mine, with the lightest touch, like a butterfly taking a quick break on a flower. "I knew I had feelin's for you, but I wasn't expectin' them to hit this hard so soon. And I need you to know how I feel."

"Blaze..."

"Don't say it back if you're not there yet. It's okay. I can wait. I'd wait forever for you. You're so thoughtful. Your heart is as big as the moon on a cold night. You're a talented artist, horseman, and a devoted son. Your patience with everybody is next level and I love you. You've already made me a better person before that damn text showed up."

His kisses are probably my most favourite thing on the planet and when he keeps kissing me, it's all I can do to not climb into his arms and laugh with the euphoria that comes when a man like Blaze tells you he loves you.

"I think I've been in love with you since I first saw you."

"What?"

"You're a mystery guy too, you know. You had that cowboy swagger going on and once you let me in and I saw more of you, I knew I could be happy with you in my life. The rest of my life, to be honest. But I didn't make you a better person. You already are. You're just figuring it out now."

His mouth drops open at my admission, and I laugh.

"Blaze, don't be so shocked. I love you. I just wasn't sure if you'd get to the same place as me or not this fast. In the plane, you said I had your heart and just those words had me all loopy. It put a lot of hope in my heart that maybe I may have found my one." I laugh a little. "Maybe we should thank Ted tomorrow."

His gaze is thoughtful as he runs his hand up my arm.

"Want to share that dessert with me?"

"Now that's real love. You said you never share your crème brûlée."

"You're my only exception to that."

Blaze gathers spoons from the kitchen and after discarding our ties and loosening our shirts, we settle back on the sofa, feet propped up on the coffee table with take-out containers on our laps, and share the best dessert I've ever tasted.

"Ohmygod, how is it legal to sell chocolate cake this good?" I moan around my fork. "Seriously Blaze, we need to get dessert there every day while we're here."

He laughs and offers me a spoonful of his.

"Try this. It's earl grey crème brûlée. The sugar on top is perfection and I don't know how it tastes so good, but it does."

With his spoon in my mouth, I moan an obscene food moan again and his happy laugh rings out.

"See? Seriously food porn or somethin'. I could eat this stuff every day and never get sick of it."

"I think that's the sign of a good thing. When you can taste it every day and not get sick of it."

He goes quiet, scooping more of his dessert in his mouth and out of the corner of my eye, I notice his hands still before he sets his carton on the table and takes mine from my hands.

"Dessert will always be there and right now it's you I really want to taste. Is that okay?"

Jesus, the way he slides to the floor in front of me has the words stuck in my throat, but my hands still work and they somehow get my pants unzipped. I barely have my ass off the couch and Blaze tears them down my legs, along with my boxers.

He places tender kisses on the inside of my thighs and kisses across my sack with such a tender touch, I bite on my lip to hold back all the mushy things threatening to come out. But it's not a time for words.

His tongue traces the vein on the side of my cock as it plumps under his attention. Everywhere he teases with his lips and tongue until I'm writhing bare assed on his sofa, an inch away from begging him to hurry and let me fuck his face.

Gentle fingers trail over my heated skin, soft and delicate, unlike anything I've ever felt. And that's when I get the message through my brain that this isn't just a BJ. He's lavishing me with the care and attention of someone in love and once I allow myself to experience the emotion behind it, it drives my pleasure through the roof. Because anyone can suck a dick, but when it's backed by the connection and passion we've been cultivating between us? Holy shit, it's next level.

Somehow I unbutton my shirt while he laps and kisses and when he finally takes me in his mouth, I flop my head back with a groan. Over and over he buries his nose into my stomach, swallowing me whole and squeezing his throat around me. I melt into the cushions, letting myself enjoy what he's giving me. Showing me.

When he finally comes up for air with a shaky gasp, I slide my hand into his hair. His lips swollen, drool on his chin and eyes glazed, as he tilts his face up to me. He's the most beautiful man in the world.

At some point, Blaze unzipped his pants and, with a wince, he pushes himself up off the floor and leans over me, kissing me with a gentleness I wasn't ready for. The thunk of his belt and pants hitting the floor follows, and I shift to allow him to straddle my lap.

His cock is hard and hot against mine. Licking his palm, he holds our dicks together and rocks his hips to create just enough friction. It's this side of pleasure. Our ragged pants and whispered words of encouragement surround me in a surreal cloud of something beyond intimacy.

I'm the first to break the spell when I speak.

"Come with me Blaze. I'm right there. Please."

The words are barely across my lips when the tingles race up my spine and I shoot into his grip, spilling over to my stomach. A low groan follows from Blaze as he comes with me and both of us struggle to catch our breath.

"I think my knees might regret that." Blaze laughs into my neck.

"Maybe I could buy you some of those gardening knee pad things. That might help?" I offer with a small laugh of my own and he sits back to peer into my face.

"Thank you."

"For buying you knee pads?"

He drops his head with a small smile and laugh. "For helpin' me find myself. For believin' in me." He presses a kiss to my forehead. "For showin' me, I can love and be loved again."

I swallow, overcome by the sincerity in his voice. But even though I'm hopelessly in love with this man, I need to lighten the moment.

"So, that's a no to the knee pads? Because a guy can get used to that."

He snorts. "Come on. Let's shower and sleep. It's been a long day." He climbs off me and tosses me my shirt to mop up some mess.

It's not until I'm washing his hair he adds.

"I'd be down with knee pads. Surprise me sometime."

And the laughter that spills out of me reminds me Blaze is definitely the one for me.

CHAPTER 24

BLAZE

I crept out of bed a few hours ago, not wanting to wake River with all my tossing and turning.

It was still too early to reach out to Dan or Heather to talk, so I rummaged through the pockets of River's bag until I found the small blocks of wood and his favourite jack knife. Settling in the chair next to the window, I work on the strokes he taught me.

The smooth motions of the sharp knife through the soft wood are calming and I can focus my thoughts better. I wish I had found this little hobby years ago. It could have helped me so much with the stress of the past few years. I've only practiced a little since River first showed me what to do, but I'm getting better. That spoon will come to fruition at some point.

When the sun finally peaks over the horizon, I pause my whittling and stare out the giant pane of glass. Watching the sunrise has always been a special moment for me. Like watching the day wake up before you, a clean slate for whatever you wanted to accomplish. Today, it's a little different.

I've already quieted the bouncing thoughts, and the biggest difference is the man in my bed. River.

He's brought me love like no other has. Even though this meeting with Ted happens in a few hours and I've dealt with a lot of the lingering emotions finally, I'm mostly okay. More curious than anything, but I'm okay with seeing him. Not just because I'll have River with me. It's also because in the last twenty-four hours I've realized it's such a waste for me to keep holding on to something that may never have made me as happy as I thought it did.

"Well, this is probably one of the best sights a guy could wake up to. Two of my favourite things."

River's voice is thick with sleep and his hair is all pokey crazy from sleeping with it wet. Scratching his belly, he saunters over to me in my penthouse, looking like he owns the place and belongs here more than me. He bends to kiss me and I wrap an arm around his waist, keeping him there.

"You're *my* favourite thing." I nip his lip before releasing him, and he pecks my lips with another kiss before wandering to the kitchen.

"Please tell me there's coffee somewhere in here."

Abandoning my chair and the carving, I join him in the kitchen and open the correct cabinet for him to find an array of coffee choices for the Keurig machine.

"So, it's a lunchtime meeting, right?" He pops the pod into the machine and leans against the counter. I still can't wrap my head around River being here, in my penthouse.

"Yeah, an old diner on the other side of town. The limo will take us, and if you want, we can have lunch there if the meeting goes well."

"I could go for greasy spoon food." He grins when he notices the creamer in the fridge. "Did you get this kind stocked for me, too?"

It's just an unflavoured heavy cream I know he likes. "Yeah," I admit. "You said the cream makes the coffee and that's the one you keep in your fridge, so I asked Heather to get some."

He sips his coffee with a pleased hum as he watches me over the edge of the mug.

"Come sit with me while the sun keeps rising?" He asks.

"Of course."

Somehow we position our bodies in the chair built for one so he can drink without burning either of us and in silence we greet the sun.

Looking around the diner, I spot Ted. He notices me when he looks up from his phone and he waves like he's an old friend.

I don't wave back.

"Blaze, thank you for coming!"

He doesn't stand to meet me but his eyes immediately land on River and if I'm not mistaken, his smile fades when he notices our joined hands.

"This is my boyfriend, River. I hope you don't mind that I brought him with me."

I actually don't give a flying fuck if he does mind but my manners come out even when I don't want them to.

"Hey, man. Nice to meet you." His eyes flick up and down River's body. "So, where did you meet? His little ranch?"

River, bless him, takes his seat and stares Ted down. "I met him on his one thousand acre co-owned ranch that helps large animals and people in need, yes. The same ranch that gives back to the community whenever it can. The same ranch Blaze will build a chicken coop on one day and deliver a horse the next. He never forgets to bring the ranch hands coffee on Thursdays because he lost a bet once and rather than doing it one time, he does it every week because it makes them happy. He cares about the people on the ranch. The same ranch that's expanding and purchasing another two hundred and fifty acres to have more pastures for animals. Is that the little ranch you mean, Ted?"

River smiles sweetly and sips from the water glass at his setting before folding his hands on the table.

Ted raises an eyebrow my way. "You brought a guard dog. Impressive."

"I brought the man I love to meet my ex. I want to give you the benefit of the doubt right now about what you called me here for, but you're not makin' it easy for me to do that."

A flash of satisfaction runs through me when I notice the flicker of anger in his eyes. Although, I'm not sure what makes him more angry. The fact I said I love River or that I'm doubting his intentions for contacting me.

"I'll bite if I need to. Just saying."

River leans back, and I squeeze his thigh under the table.

"Listen, Ted, I'm not sure why you asked to see me, but it was good timin' for me, as I have somethin' I need to say."

"God, you're back to sounding like a country bumpkin again, Blaze. Why? You're at the top of the business world. You can take this even further with the right connections. I can help you."

"Actually, you can't help me. And I'm sorry you don't like the way I sound but it's who I am."

Ted leans across the table jostling the glasses. "You could be an even bigger billionaire. You were at the top of this in North America, Blaze. I have contacts to get you all over the world. We could be so good together, baby. I asked to see you because my friend needs help with a business and I knew you were the right guy to call. But if you're back to slumming it with farmers, I might have to rescind my offer."

Again he tosses a disgusted look towards River and I see red.

"I never want to do business with you or anyone like you. Or anyone you know. I don't even want to be in the same room as you right now. But I'll tell you why I came here today. It wasn't for you, it was for me."

"You? If you showed up alone, I would've believed that."

"Were you hopin' to take advantage of my good nature again?"

Ted bites his cheek as he lets his gaze dart between River and me. "I was hoping you were down to fuck. I won't lie." He laughs when River growls under breath. "But I also need money and if you won't do business with me, I'll have to find someone else."

"You seriously made that whole plea up just to get me here to ask for money?"

"It worked, didn't it? Shame you brought a tag-along. Unless you're into sharing now?"

Ted flashes a smirk towards River.

"Absolutely not." River grits out.

Ted stands to leave, but I reach out to grasp his wrist.

"I have one question. Why me? Was it always just because of the money?"

He takes so long to answer that I'm not sure he will.

"I cared about you in the beginning. But I cared more about the lifestyle and the money. When the next pretty face came by and flirted, I didn't say no. I took your money because you made it easy for me to take. I should've left you, but it was easier to stay and keep taking." I let his wrist go as he straightens himself up. "You were hoping for some kind of answer, then? Maybe I called because I was begging for forgiveness?" He laughs with a shake of his head. "I hate to disappoint you, Blaze. I'm not asking for forgiveness because I'm not even sorry."

Ted turns to River with a sleazy grin, and I wonder what I ever saw in this guy. The power I let him have over me makes me sick. "If you're good, he'll just tell you to take money out whenever you want to. When he passes you the bank card, just say thank you. He literally never checks."

He winks at River and my guy launches to his feet. With light-ning fast hands, he grabs a fistful of Ted's shirt and pulls him close to him. Ted's hip bounces off the hard edge of the table and a nearby table falls silent, watching it all unfold.

"You're a real piece of shit and while I'd love to throw a punch and mess up your face, I'd rather say thank you instead. So, thank you for being an asshole and letting this magnificent human go, and thank you for making it easy for me to dislike you." He shoves him away, Ted stumbles but recovers. River gnashes in the air towards him like an angry dog. "This guard dog says get the fuck out of here before I change my mind and bite for real."

Ted doesn't even say goodbye and saunters out of the restaurant, sliding the high end sunglasses I probably paid for on as he leaves without a final look back.

"Well, that went well."

River slides next to me. "Are you okay?"

"I'm... totally fine? Like, I was hopin' he wanted to, I dunno, maybe apologize, but that was secondary."

River slips his hand into mine and gently turns my face to his.

"If nothing else, you hopefully figured out he was the problem, and not you? You're not somebody's trash, Blaze. You're the whole package and you don't need money for that. He's garbage, and he took advantage of you because he knew you cared about him and trusted him. Don't let him be the one to break you."

"No, he didn't. This was an eye opener. I mean, I know I overlooked a lot of his behaviour, but he just showed me the real Ted. That wasn't the same guy I met and fell for. Not even close. I guess he fooled me?" With a sigh, I take his hand from my face, kissing his palm. "I'm partially responsible for ignorin' the signs, but in the end, he's not a good person, and that's no reflection on me."

"No, it's not. He's horrible, Blaze. I can't believe he asked you here for more money and a roll in the hay. While pretending there was something serious going on with him because he knew you'd not be able to say no. Who does that?"

I laugh when he scrunches up his face in disgust. "People who don't want to acknowledge the face in the mirror every day and maybe someone who isn't happy with themself."

"Do you want to get out of here? Order some take out and just stay in?"

"If that's what you want to do, then yes."

His brown eyes meet mine and holy hell, this man. "I want to do you, over and over, in fact. But a man's gotta eat." He winks and flags the server down. "And I want a cheeseburger, but I'd rather get out of this place so I can enjoy it. The lingering presence of that man makes me want to puke. I can't believe you'd ever be with him. He probably chews with his mouth open or picks his nose. Some disgusting habit, I'm sure."

He rattles off his order to the server and, without asking, orders me the same thing. When he turns back to me, I let my body shake with a laugh.

"You're jealous? Really?"

"He's like a walking Ken doll. Of course I'm jealous." He grumbles and while I want to assure him he's the best man for me, I also sort of like he has a protective side.

"He's got nothing on you, Riv. You have my heart. I wasn't lyin'. And thinkin' back, I don't think I ever gave it to Ted. I may have thought I did, but I didn't. Because it feels nothin' like how I feel now."

I seem to keep having revelations about myself in the presence of food. The server sets our take-out bag on the table and River handles the bill.

"And how do you feel now?" He asks with that perfectly adorable grin.

"Like I finally found what I've been lookin' for."

CHAPTER 25

RIVER

"Is she going to be okay?"

The last few weeks have been a blur with the influx of rescue animals. Since Blaze and I returned from our whirlwind trip to Rosevale, we've barely had time to ourselves. But I'm okay with that. Because it's days like today I'm reminded of how much good the ranch does for animals with no other option.

The new draft being unloaded is a malnourished Percheron named Honey. I want to be angry with the previous owner but I'm too concerned about her well-being to waste energy on anger.

Blaze coaxes her with a gentle voice to a stall we enlarged just for her. It takes twice as long as normal to get her there. Honey's eyes are wild and scared and her short huffs paired with her frequent stopping and freezing keep me on edge. She may be weak but she's still large enough to hurt someone if things were to go sideways.

"She'll be just fine once she lets us take care of her. Won't you girl?"

Blaze's voice soothes her, and she allows him to run a hand down her neck. Dan quietly slides next to me as we watch Blaze work his magic with the skittish horse.

"He just has a way to get through to them when they're scared. I don't know what it is, but he's soothed and settled nearly every draft in this barn. You should've seen him with Dexter."

"Who's Dexter?"

"A horse my grandpa had. He was a great horse, but we had a thunderstorm out in the field once and heavy wind brought down a tree. Poor Dex was just in the wrong place at the wrong time. He spooked and ran into the barbed fence and cut himself up pretty bad."

Honey puffs and tries to rear, but Blaze, ever steady, pets her and speaks softly at her side. His hand is both firm on the lead and gentle on her body. Her breathing slows, and she takes a few steps forward again.

"Blaze was the only one he let treat his wounds or get close to him for a few weeks. Even the clatter of feed pails spooked him for a while. He blindly trusted Blaze for anything and when he was better, it was like the accident never even happened."

"Well, I can see the blind trust thing. Soothing, hand. Gentle voice."

Another gift Blaze has but failed to take credit for. His way with the heavy horses is a thing of beauty. Seeing him with any of these gentle giants always makes my heart take flight. Anyone with a set of eyes can see how much he cares about them and when they return the affection, it's truly an amazing sight.

Honey finally reaches the opening to her new and improved home and once she's secure, he doesn't just walk away. He stays and keeps speaking to her, offering a hand to sniff or have a scratch. His gentle murmurs reach the horse and she slows her pacing to stand close to the door. Blaze slides his hand down her neck and her muscles no longer twitch.

"I could watch him with horses all day."

Dan hums in agreement. "He's definitely worth watching. I'll give you that." Dan shifts, bringing his mouth closer to my ear. "I know tonight is a big night for you two. I don't normally talk about our conversations, but he came to me this morning. He's really nervous. More than I've ever seen him."

"Shit, really?"

"Yeah, but also? He's excited about what's to come. Just be patient if he derails a little tonight. He's not going to run. Since he took you to Rosevale, he's much better at accepting the good that comes his way. Once it's out of the way, he'll relax. And River?"

"Yeah?"

"I've never heard Blaze talk about anyone the way he does you. He's a man in love and he's yours."

Dan claps me on the shoulder and meanders out of the barn. Leaving me alone to watch Blaze in action. I don't know how much time has passed, but when Blaze finally leaves Honey's stall and finds me still there, the brightness of his smile sends shivers through my body.

"Hey. Have you been watchin' this whole time?"

Removing his Stetson, he leans in to press a kiss to my lips before straightening again.

"I like to watch you with the horses. I don't think you're aware, but when you spend time with them like that, anyone can see what kind of person you are."

Hooking his fingers into my belt loops, he pulls me up against him with a smile.

"And what kind of person do you see, Riv?"

"A man worth taking home to meet parents and sharing my life with. A man with a heart so big it's a wonder how it can stay in your body. Someone kind who searches for special ways to connect."

"You see all that watchin' me talk to a horse?"

"Yup."

His smile is crooked, and he shakes his head, a slight flush to his cheeks.

"I think you're delusional."

"No, just a man in love."

"I didn't know you were this cheesy."

"Hey, you wanted romance. I'm just telling you like it is. I'm picking you up tonight. You still good with early?"

"You could show up at 3 A.M and I'd still be ready."

With a lingering kiss, I gently remove his fingers from my belt loops and step back.

"I won't be late, Blaze. Might even be early, so don't make me wait."

I spin on my heel and walk back to my truck. If I turn around, I might spend too much time finding a dark corner in the barn and showing him how much I'm so damn head over heels in love with him.

Not that he doesn't already know.

But I like to show my feelings often. Naked.

It's much more fun than saying it with a card.

Should I wear a tie?

No. Too formal. Blaze said he likes not being in a suit. Slipping the tie off, I hang it back in the closet and chew my thumb.

But it's a special occasion. My boyfriend is meeting my dad for the first time and we're joining him at his retirement home for an early Christmas dinner. It's a big deal.

I should wear a tie.

I grab another one and loop it around my neck. The red one, I think. While I don't own a full suit, we left the one Heather picked out for me at the condo in case we go back; I have a blazer. So it's country style. My favourite jeans, a button-up shirt with a tie and a blazer. This feels right.

The only person I'm trying to impress is Blaze and, really, I don't even have to do that.

And now that I'm ready, my palms are sweaty and my stomach is tight.

I've been looking forward to this night since Blaze agreed he was ready to meet my dad. Originally we planned to do this as soon as we returned. We were both excited about it and my dad wants to meet the man I'm in love with. But the ranch needed all hands on deck. We were swamped with new horses who needed care, many of them responding best to Blaze so he put in extra time to make sure each one was okay. Then poor Mando ate something he shouldn't have and Blaze didn't want to leave him alone until he was sure the cat would recover.

Now we're in the thick of the holiday season and it's finally worked out for them to meet.

Until three minutes ago I was excited, and now, I want to puke. What the hell is wrong with me?

I know I've been absent from my best friend, but I need her reassurance.

Dialing Kelly's number, I hope she's not buried in a meeting. When she answers, I smile at the sound of her voice.

"Hello my almost invisible friend who only calls lately when he needs date advice."

"Uh, yeah. Sorry. Last time, I swear, and then we'll make plans to meet up."

"You owe me a pitcher of margaritas and all-you-can-eat tacos."

"Done."

"And an extra Christmas gift because I'm salty you missed our meeting last month."

"I've been a horrible friend. I'm sorry. We're making plans and keeping them this weekend if you're in town."

"You're lucky I love you. Yes, I'll be in town and I'd love to see you. I might forget what you look like, though. It's been so long you should make sure you wear a name tag to the restaurant."

"Ouch. I deserved that. You know I love you though, right?"

"Yeah, yeah. I know and I'm just teasing you, but seriously I need a margarita meltdown so we're doing it. So what's today's emergency?"

"I'm bringing Blaze to meet dad tonight and while that shouldn't be a big deal, I started freaking out. Like, I don't even know how to describe it, but I'm... fuck, I need to change my shirt. I'm sweating that bad."

"Why though? Your dad is seriously one of the best people I know. Maybe you've got a fever for love."

She snort laughs and I laugh along with her.

"He is. It's not dad. I'm just... Kelly, I've never brought anyone home before. What if dad doesn't like him?"

"If your dad doesn't like him, he's in a terrible mood or there's actually something wrong with the guy."

"Well, that's not helpful at all."

There's chatter in the background and her phone muffles.

"Listen Riv, nerves are fine and my best advice is to imagine them naked."

"You want me to think of my eighty-something dad and my boyfriend naked at the same time? That's... only helpful to lose my appetite."

"But you're no longer nervous. Thank me later. I gotta run. Work needs me. Don't forget tacos!"

She ends the call and I'm left shaking my head with a smile. But she's right. My dad will love anyone I bring home. He knows all about Blaze and has been asking when he can meet him. Maybe I'm nervous about Blaze not liking my dad.

Whatever it is giving me this whole weird vibe needs to fuck off. Because aside from the day I met Blaze, tonight will be one of the best days of my life.

Now sitting in Blaze's driveway, I have replaced my nervousness with excitement. I considered how much I should do before and after this dinner, but in the end, I knew I wanted to just make us both smile.

I also know I couldn't wait until tonight to give him his surprise.

Arranging spring flowers in December when there's already a dusting of snow on the ground is no easy feat. Thankfully, the woman I know with the greenhouse was more than happy to help me out and she forced the bulbs for me. He's going to love them.

Rounding the truck, I somehow wrangle out the ridiculously large bouquet of daffodils with no damage and since I can't hide them behind my back like the cheesy heroes in the movies, I settle for hiding my face behind them until he opens the door.

"Oh my god, River. How...,"

He trails off as I push the mass of daffodils to him.

"Hold that thought."

I rush back to get the box from the back seat and return to find Blaze still speechless in the doorway.

"Close the door, babe. We don't want Mando getting out."

The cat in question sits in the hallway but shows no interest in going outside. With a chirp, he winds around my legs a few times in greeting before returning to the living room. Probably to watch his TV.

"God, there's like two dozen daffodils here, River. I don't have a vase big enough."

I pat the box I've set on the hallway bench. "I've got it covered. We have some time, so I'll help you."

Carrying the box to the kitchen, I set it on the island and start unpacking the dozen glass milk bottles inside.

"These are perfect for their short stems. I had the lady who grew the flowers paint them for me. Well, her daughter helped. I think they turned out quite nice, and it gave them an idea for next year's flower market. And she tied —"

"River."

I turn to find Blaze behind me in the kitchen. His eyes are shiny and his lips move, but no words come out.

"Blaze? What's wrong?"

With a shaky sigh, he finally steps closer, cradling the bouquet like it's a newborn baby.

"You asked the flower lady to grow daffodils for me? In time for Christmas?"

"I did."

He takes one of the painted milk bottles off the counter before gently placing it back down. "And you had all these bottles painted for them because you knew I'd need more than one vase?"

"Um, yeah? But also because you said daffodils bring you joy and remind you of a happy time. So if I brought you lots, you could have them all over the house. Then everywhere you go, you'd be happy. If I remember right, you also said they signal new beginnings and I think if there's ever a time for that kind of symbolism, it's tonight."

Gently, he places the bouquet next to the bottles and cradles my face with his palms.

"Thank you. This is... thoughtful and so sweet. Nobody has ever done this for me before. It definitely makes me happy."

He feathers a kiss so soft to my forehead I almost don't feel it. But that's what makes it so good with us. If he physically touches me or not, I know we're connected.

"You're welcome. You make it easy for me to do nice things for you, Blaze. And you deserve it. So much."

Dropping his forehead to mine, he stays there for a moment and it breaks my heart to know he's so overwhelmed by what I think is a simple gesture you do for people you love. Sure, I planned and asked a local greenhouse to force them out of season. The bottles too I planned, but... I just wanted to make him smile and let him know I always think of him. A guy like Blaze should always know how much he's thought of. Since we took the trip to the city and we bonded more than I ever thought possible, he's tattooed on my brain. And my heart. No matter whatever happens between us, this man will always own a piece of me.

"I love you." He sighs before kissing me again and wiping a stray tear away. "I'll help get these into water. I don't want to keep your dad waitin'."

Blaze straightens all the little bows tied to the bottles and fills them with water and plant food while I measure and cut the stems, placing a few of them into each bottle. When we're done, Blaze leaves them all in the kitchen for now and we'll place them around the house later.

He says goodbye to Mando and turns on his cat TV to Meerkat Manor before piling some treats on the floor for him.

"Be a good cat. We'll be back soon."

With a final goodbye to Mando, he locks the door and we're on the way to meet my dad.

Chapter 26

Blaze

Y ou'd think by the time you're forty, you may have met the parents of a partner at least once.

But not me.

I didn't date in high school. When I got to college, it was a few experiments, nothing serious. Once I was an adult and tried the dating scene, nothing ever lasted more than a month tops before we went our separate ways. With Ted, the only time we brought the topic up was when I revealed my whole childhood and he was so disgusted it never came up again.

I haven't had parents since I was a child. The only significant person I'd ever want a partner to meet is Dan. He's the closest thing I have to a brother, and River already works for him. So there's no one else for him to meet. When I asked Dan what it was like to meet Martin's parents, he just smiled in that dazed kind of way he has when he talks about Martin. He said they're who made the love of his life, so he can't help but love them too. Or some other Zen shit Dan was good at.

"Are you waiting for me to open your door now all the time, or are you going to get out?"

"I don't know. I kinda like it when you do things for me."

"There are lots of things I'd like to do to you. That's correct."

"I said do *for* me, Mr.McAdams. You have a filthy mind."

He wiggles his eyebrows. "And you love it."

"I won't deny it." Opening the door, I slide out and meet him at the front of the truck, where he takes my hand in his.

"We sign in at the front desk and I'll take you to dad's room where we'll visit for a bit. Then we all go to the dining room. There's a special turkey dinner being served. Lots of residents here invite their families over for it. Some of them don't have great mobility and this is much easier on them. They still get to be with families and it's like a big party."

"Okay. It sounds great."

"You sure? You sound like you'd rather walk over crushed glass."

"I've never met the parents before. But I want to meet your dad. I'm nervous. What if he doesn't like me?"

"He's really looking forward to meeting you. He'll love you because I love you."

River's confidence in this one simple thing that's so monumental to me doesn't go unnoticed. He's told me so much about both of his parents over the past few months that I feel like I already know his dad. No picture River has ever painted of him is grounds for me to believe the man won't like me or disapprove of where I came from.

But that doesn't mean I can't still be nervous to meet his remaining parent.

Taking my hand again after signing us in, he leads me down a bright hallway. We pass several staff members and a few residents, all of whom know River, and greet him by name with a smile. One resident wants him to stop by and help with her crossword, but he politely steps around the request, promising to come back another time.

"Are you the crossword king here at the retirement home?"

"Hey, don't let the granny appearance fool you. Some of these ladies are ruthless. Don't even get me started on their Scrabble games."

Stopping in front of a door with a giant Rudulph the Red-Nosed Reindeer poster on it, he places his hand on the door-knob. "This is it. Last chance to back out."

"Never. You're it for me, Riv. I'm ready to meet your dad."

Opening the door, he calls out to his dad, who is sitting in his recliner and he doesn't even have to turn my way for me to know he will become one of my favourite people. The smile in his voice is just like River's.

"Hello, son! Come in!"

River tugs me into the small space, and his dad pushes himself up to grab his walker. The smile on his face is like seeing River in another forty years and the man beams at his son.

"Dad, this is Blaze. The one I've been telling you about."

His dad shuffles over to where we stand near the door. "It's a pleasure to finally meet you. River can't stop talking about you. I was wondering if you were real or if he was just trying to humour his old man."

He perches himself on the walker and grins up at me.

"The pleasure is mine, Mr.McAdams. I'm so happy to meet you."

"You can call me Ray. No need to be formal. Unless you want to ask for his hand in marriage or something like that."

"Dad!"

River groans and his dad and I share a laugh at his expense.

"Hey, can you help me tie this tie?"

"What happened to your clip on one?"

"It's not the time for that one. I want a special one. It's not every day I get to meet my son's boyfriend."

His smile at me is so warm, it's like he's wrapped me in a hug instead. Reaching for his tie, I look at River with my unspoken question. His face softens, and he nods for me to go ahead.

"I used to tie a tie every day for my old job. I can do this in the dark, Ray, if you don't mind."

"River said you used to own a business. I looked you up."

My fingers move slower than needed as I glance up at his watery blue eyes. "Did you? I hope what you found passed the test."

"Your company gave substantial donations every year to the women's hospital in Rosevale and to the Boys and Girls Club in Bloomburg. You also sold your company for millions less than its appraised value."

My fingers smooth the tie with a slight shake, and I adjust the knot for him. "That's all true, yes."

Ray's eyes smile without even trying and I stuff my hands in my pockets, unsure of where he's going with all this. If he found out that much, he must have read the reasons I did somewhere, too.

"For a man who tries to hide who he really is, you're not doing it well, my boy."

"Dad, don't —"

"It's okay Riv. It's nothin' you don't already know about me."

"I hope you keep my son's heart as safe as you do the memory of people you love. He's a good man and I couldn't be more proud of who he's chosen to spend his life with."

All Ray has done is search me on Google, true. But you had to go deeper to find about the whys of those donations. I didn't make them public, but they are a public record in the company's financials. He's done well to comb through all the garbage in a statement to find them.

"You know, I would've just told you anythin' you wanted to know. You didn't need to sneak around and google me."

I reach out a hand to adjust his tie again as it sits askew on his shirt and a smile fills his wrinkled face.

"Well, an old man has to fill his days somehow. And I wanted to be prepared. Besides, I can only take so many games of strip Scrabble before it grows old."

River groans again, and Ray and I laugh.

"Daadd, please tell them to stop that. I won't help anymore if I know they're just luring you over there for their enjoyment. This is supposed to be a retirement home, not the set of seniors gone wild."

River holds the door open, and we leave the apartment to walk to the dining hall.

"If you think naked Scrabble is going wild, I may have to warn Blaze to run in the other direction."

River walks alongside Ray as he moves slowly with his walker. I trail behind them, partly because of the width of the hallway but also to have a moment to myself. Ray is a wonderful man and River is a carbon copy of him with the eyes and smile and easygoing attitude. Watching them laugh and walk together squeezes my heart in a different way.

An opportunity I never had was to be both close to my father and to watch him grow old. Even if I had tried to stay behind and help, it wouldn't have changed the person he was. But it changed me. For years I thought it was a change for the bad, but maybe there's good in there too. I couldn't help my dad, but I helped myself along with many other people over the years. Most through donations, Ray discovered, because it was the only way I knew how.

It's funny how the decisions we make when we're younger follow us as adults. Even when they seem so small and centered around us. There's truly a ripple effect.

River hangs back as his dad finds his seat at the table for us.

"He likes you. Are you okay?"

"I've never been better. He's wonderful. You're a lot like him."

"I'll take that as a compliment. My dad's a good man."

"What about you? Why were you so nervous? Did you know he googled me?"

"I didn't know he did that! I was more nervous about what you'd think of him, maybe? I don't really know. I think I was worried you might not like him and you'd not want to deal with that in your life. Because he's part of the package and it scared me, you might not want that."

"River...," I cup his cheek with my palm. "He could be the monster of all fathers and I'd still want you in my life. You're worth havin' over any kind of colourful family member. Look where I came from. I was worried your dad would think I wasn't good enough for you."

He leans in and places a soft kiss on my lips. "You're the best one for me, Blaze. I'm so happy I finally offered to teach you to whittle."

"Me too."

His dad calls across the dining room to come and sit and we make our way through the residents to join him.

It's festive and fun and I've not celebrated the Christmas season with so many people before. Maybe ever. And I don't even know them, but somehow, every stranger in this building is a friend.

There's indeed a turkey dinner with all the fixings served and for dessert, they placed trays of home-baked cookies at every table. One of the staff made all the cookies herself, which was a super nice thing to do. We enjoy the cookies and coffee while a children's choir sings carols and some of the staff perform a quick Night Before Christmas skit, changing the words to tease staff members.

Ray laughs loud and deep and when he catches River's eye, the smile he returns to his dad makes my heart beat all wonky.

At the end of the evening, it's only 8 P.M, but Ray is sagging hard. We take him back to his apartment and River helps him with his tie and getting out of his dress clothes.

"I hope you enjoyed yourself, Blaze. It was so nice to meet you finally. I can see why River is so in love with you. You're a nice man with a firm handshake."

A laugh squeaks out as I smile at the man who won a piece of my heart just as easy as his son did.

"Thank you. I've had a great night and I'm happy to have met you too. River speaks highly of you."

"You know, I'm very lucky to have a son as good as him. He's the most precious thing in my life. When his mother died, I worried so much about him and how life might be difficult for him. He was always a sensitive kid, picking flowers and trying to save all the animals who wandered into our yard. He has the biggest heart."

River places a glass of juice next to his dad with a small bowl of popcorn.

"You're embarrassing me just a little, dad."

Ray brushes off River's gentle scolding.

"A parent always worries about their child, no matter how old they get. And I always want you to have the life you deserve. The love you deserve. I think you found someone special, and it makes me happy."

River settles on my lap in the other easy chair. Ray only has room for the two chairs in his tiny place, and I'm certainly not complaining. I wrap my arms around River. "I think I found someone special, too."

River stares into my eyes before dropping a kiss on my nose. "I love you." He whispers.

"An old man wouldn't be offended if you want to go home. I've got popcorn and the National Geographic channel."

River fusses over things for a few more minutes. I say my goodbye to Ray and step into the hallway so they can have a private conversation. I don't know if they need it, but I'll give it to them, anyway.

He finds me in the hallway, reading a bulletin board of announcements for the residents. I laugh when I notice Scrabble in the lounge is cancelled until further notice.

River slips his hand in mine and we make our way back to his truck. We don't hurry, neither of us in a rush to end the evening and basking in this new level of intimacy between us. It was just a simple dinner with his dad, but somehow it's more than that. Tonight it feels like I'm now a member of this tiny family and it overflows my heart. Before I can open the passenger side door, he spins me around and kisses me until I'm gasping for air and clawing at his clothes to bring him closer.

"Thank you." He breathes against my shoulder.

"For what? Lettin' you kiss me like that in the parking lot of a retirement home?"

"For everything now and for everything you'll be."

We hang onto each other for a few moments until he finally breaks away and opens the door for me.

I was already madly and deeply in love with this man, but now things have shifted.

Thinking of everything I will be for him and everything he means to me steals my breath. It's no longer something I'm afraid of.

And I want it to last forever.

CHAPTER 27

RIVER

February

I t's become our thing, this sleigh ride and the experience we take people on.

I don't know if it's the romantic winter wonderland of it or just Blaze and I together making our riders laugh and have fun, but it's more than just sitting on a sleigh and being dragged along the snow. I've gladly met him out here on the coldest of winter days to do this when I could've stayed bundled in bed. His joy from being with his horses, his girls, as he likes to call them, is infectious. So it became our thing because the man I love with his favourite horses is something I never want to miss.

Blaze asked me today to join him on Honey's first official hitch. She's gained weight since arriving at the ranch a few months ago and Blaze has worked tirelessly with her. He thinks she must have been used to pull in her previous life because she took to it like a duck to water. Although, I also think Honey would do just about anything for Blaze. He's paired her with his favourite Percheron Thunder. Thunder, unlike her name, is calm and the perfect horse to partner with Honey.

The sounds of hooves crunching on snow and jingle bells pull my eyes to the barn as Blaze brings the team out to the waiting sleigh. Their braided manes and tails have little red rosettes in them as if they're going to a horse show. Guess that explains why he beat me to the ranch today.

Pulling the team to a stop in front of the sleigh, he beams a smile at me. "Surprise! I made them look pretty for you today."

He clucks softly and moves them back towards the sleigh's hitch. Once in place, I steady the horses as Blaze attaches all their hooks and... you know what? I don't even know what all the parts are called and I should probably learn. But he's such an expert with it all and moves so effortlessly doing it, I never want to interrupt and ask questions. Because seeing him in his element is incredible. He was made to be here and I'll never tire of watching him.

Blaze passes the reins up to me after I've hopped up on the sleigh.

"I'll be right back!"

He jogs back to the main farmhouse and I'm left with the team, wondering what the hell he's up to. When he exits Dan's place with a giant picnic basket in his arms, I can only laugh. With a mischief filled smile on his face, he slides the basket between our feet and hops up beside me.

"Don't peek. It's a surprise."

Taking the reins from me, he urges the team onto the trail we usually take and I squeeze over next to him on the driver's bench.

"A surprise in a picnic basket. Is it food?"

"Maybe."

"So it might not be food?"

"You'll just have to wait and find out."

He leans over for a kiss and I oblige. The sun gleams off the crisp snow and the black horses against the white background with the pops of red in their manes are worthy of a calendar cover.

"You should braid their manes every ride. It's pretty. Gives it an extra special feeling."

"Oh? Does it feel extra special today for you, then?"

"Kind of. But I know how long it takes for you to make them look like that. So, yeah, it's extra special."

He beams a smile again. "Good. That's what I was hopin' for."

I know I'm in good hands and whatever he's up to, I'll find out soon. Until then I'll try to keep my curiosity in check and enjoy this rare weekend day together. We've both been so busy with work on the ranch and our days off we've spent them either in my workshop as Blaze helps me with a few custom orders or snuggled on his couch with Mando in the evenings.

So an afternoon out together like this has been a long time coming.

We draw closer to the fire pit stop, and there's a fire already burning.

"You sent someone ahead to start the fire for us?"

"I did. I didn't want to spend the time doing it myself, so I asked for help."

He draws the team to a stop in the usual spot and, after securing the team; he offers his hand to me. When I take it, he pulls me close to him and kisses me so slowly I melt into him.

"The first of your surprises is waitin'. C'mon."

He grabs the basket from the sleigh and leads me back into the trees that surround our little clearing. The sleigh riders often walk around back here to take pictures and marvel at the size of some trees. On windy days, it provides some relief from the cold winter winds.

"Stand right here."

I do as he asks and cock my head as he walks ahead of me. I hear a muffled *aha!* and laugh out loud. But the laughter dies when he pulls out a small table and two chairs. They're just tiny, like the patio furniture people put on their condo balconies and Blaze opens them before securing them in a semi snow packed area.

Walking back to me, he picks up the basket again and takes my hand, leading me to the table.

"Curious yet?"

"I was curious when you brought the basket out and told me not to peek."

He tries to take the little chair out for me, but it's stuck in the snow. "Just sit. I'll move the table instead."

After juggling the table, the basket, and the other chair, he sits next to me. I'm hoping it's time to see what's in the basket, but he pops off the chair.

"I almost forgot!"

He walks back to the tree where he found the table and chairs and a loud hum fills the air. It sounds like a small generator. When the hundreds of twinkling lights come alive, up in our secluded little forest, my suspicions of a generator are confirmed, and I wonder how I didn't notice all the lights before.

Blaze settles next to me, breathless and smiling. "Surprise number one. Do you like it?"

I'd prefer not having the noise of the generator in the background, but I can't deny it's beautiful. And beyond romantic.

"It's gorgeous, Blaze. When did you find time to organize this?"

"Oh, I had help. It might be my idea, but I had several helpers to make this all happen."

"I love it."

Leaning over, I press a light kiss to his lips. "But I'm dying to know what's in the basket."

He unloads forks and napkins and sets them on the table first. The napkins have cute little candy hearts with professions of love on them, and I suddenly realize this must be an early Valentine's date. Shit. All I got him was a card with a promise of sex in the love shower.

"Close your eyes, Riv."

I do as I'm told again, and there's some rustling. The table jiggles, and he swears under his breath. I laugh out loud and he shushes me.

"Okay. Open your eyes."

"Oh my god. Blaze... is this... is this dessert from that place in the city?"

"Yeah. I had to work some major supply issues to get it here, but in the end there's literally nothing UPS won't overnight ship."

"Wouldn't it have been easier to just go to the city ourselves?"

His brow furrows. "Would you have preferred that? I didn't think you wanted to go back there anytime soon, and I thought this would be a better option for you."

"Oh, god. I'm sorry. I sound like an asshole. I didn't mean it the way it sounded. You're a million times right. This is so much better and it can't get any more romantic than this."

"I bet it can." He winks and feeds me a spoonful of the crème brûlée he got me addicted to.

What else could he possibly try to pull out of his sleeve that would top this already? Hell, I was happy to just be on the sleigh by ourselves. Everything else is just a bonus.

The February day is crisp and being away from the fire in his little grove of trees, while ultra romantic, is getting chilly. Blaze notices when I snuggle closer with a shiver.

"I forgot to bring the extra blanket. So it's not completely perfect."

"I've got you to keep me warm, though. Pretty good plan B."

I wiggle my eyebrows and move closer to him.

"Or we could stand by the fire. It's why it's there. I knew this would be chilly, but I really wanted to try this twinkle light thing."

"It's beautiful and worth every bit of thought and effort. I need to take pictures."

I snap a few of us together with my phone in this fairyland setting and Blaze packs up the stuff from the table.

"Um, are you too cold here for real? Or do you want to go to the fire for the rest?"

"I'm okay. I'll follow your plan, Blaze. A little cold never hurt me before."

"Good. Okay. Um, well... ," He laughs softly. "This is the part where I get nervous."

He removes his glove and fishes in his coat pocket.

"So, um. I made this for you."

Blaze hands me a spoon. Not just any spoon. He carved it and tied a little red bow on it. It's the most perfect spoon to ever be a spoon.

"I know it's not perfect, but —"

"Are you kidding me? It couldn't be more perfect. You made it yourself. For me. And you didn't ask for any help because I don't recognize the wood."

"Well, I snuck it from your stash so it's your wood." He snickers and I roll my eyes. "But... okay... I need to ask you something."

Blaze's face flushes, and he inhales. "I love you. I love everythin' about you and us. It's been an eye openin' few months for me. When I first came here, I was lost. I didn't know who I was anymore. Everythin' was upside down. But you, River, you've turned me right side up."

"Blaze... I don't know what to say. Until I met you, I thought my life was fine the way it was. Then you came and lit up my days like nothing else. You're so thoughtful and you give the best kisses I've ever had."

"I'd let that go straight to my head if I knew you kissed more than a handful of men. But I'll still take it."

He kisses me then. Proof that he can make my heart flutter and bring me to my knees just by placing his lips on mine.

"That spoon took me a long time. I made several, but I kept two. The second one I gave to your dad yesterday."

"You went to see my dad?"

"Several times now."

"He never said anything to me."

"Because I asked him not to. Not until after today."

I don't know what he's getting at and he's once again reaching into his pocket and he hands me a folded up envelope.

Opening it, I scan the documents and drawings, and I'm not sure what I'm looking at. I turn to him with questions in my eyes.

Taking the papers from my hand, he explains.

"We spend a lot of evenins' in your workshop and they're some of my favourite nights. Then we come home to my place because I don't like leaving Mando by himself too much. Those are my favourite nights too. I'd like to have that all in one place." He places the top paper on the table. "This is a plan to move your existing workshop. I talked to your dad about it. He wasn't sure if you were more attached to the building or just the stuff inside, since your mom made sure you had it all with her life insurance." He moves to the second paper. "This is a plan to build a new shop, or place the existing one on my property."

He clears his throat and locks his gaze with mine. "It's a really complicated way of askin' you to move in with me, River. Because I want all of our favourite things in one place, but I don't want to dishonour the memory of your mom."

This man.

"What do I do with my house?"

"Whatever you like. We could fix it up and sell it or rent it."

Shuffling the papers around, I notice he has dates scheduled for either option. When foundation would be poured, how a service would lift my building onto a float and move it. He's thought of everything and, of course, he has. I recall sitting by mom's bedside for all those long days and how she told me about the workshop plan for me. She wanted that to be my plan for life. She knew that's where I was most comfortable. But do I need those same walls to still honour my mom's wishes?

"What did my dad seem to think?"

"Heh, well, your dad seems to think you don't need to work out of a buildin' to be close to her. And I may have made him cry a little."

"You made my dad cry!?"

"Hey, he made me cry first. I gave him the spoon to show him what you taught me and how much you mean to me. We talked a long time about your projects and how amazin' you are. He told me about all the whittlin' you had done and how your mom wanted you happy after she was gone. And then he said, Blaze, anyone would be proud to call you their son or partner. I'm very happy my River met you. That's when I cried."

I knew Blaze was someone I could fall hard for even before I invited him over that first night. Once he discovered he was worthy of every good thing that came to him, he blossomed in our relationship. He held nothing back, and I was the lucky recipient. From helping me in the shop to bringing me coffee in the morning to kisses all day long, he's the love of my life. And I wasn't even looking for it.

"First, I'm upset because you're making me cry, being all thoughtful and romantic. That's my job."

He laughs and wipes away my stray tears. "But most of all, I'm incredibly thankful you rode into this ranch and stabbed me in the hand. Blaze, you are without a doubt the perfect match for me. You could have just asked me to move in, but you considered the background of my shop and that... that's the single most thoughtful thing anyone has ever done."

I have to kiss him then and I do, taking his face in my hands and peppering soft kisses all over his face.

"Yes, I'll move in with you. Can I start tonight?"

He laughs with the release of breath. "Oh thank god. Yes, we can start right now, even."

Dragging me back to the sleigh while lugging the basket, I make him stop by the bonfire.

"As romantic as all this, love alone does not keep me warm."

"You know, the best way to get warm is skin to skin with another person. Under covers. Inside."

"You drive a hard bargain." I rush towards the sleigh. "Make these horses giddy up!"

CHAPTER 28

BLAZE

The moonlight shines through my bedroom window and lands across River's sleeping face. After rushing back to take care of the horses, Heath was still hanging around after cleaning up the lights for me. He offered to finish up with them since he knew what I asked River. He was the biggest help of all making yesterday special for River. When I mentioned in passing how I wanted to have a unique date to ask River a special question, Heath had a digital file for me the next day.

He made a Pinterest board and outlined several ideas based on what he knew about both of us. He may be clumsy as hell, but I think he's found his calling with event planning. Maybe even wedding planning because the kid has a hidden romantic side. Next week, I'm reporting back to Martin about what he did and we'll see if we can steer him to something more aligned with his strengths. He's a great worker on the ranch and loves the animals, but it's not the best use of his skills.

But now I'm in bed with the single most important person in my life. When I came here, what feels like a million years ago now and left the city behind, finding the happiness I have with River wasn't something I thought I'd ever find. Mainly because I didn't think I was worthy of such great love, but also, I wasn't sure what it was I needed.

If anyone was ever lost in the sea of life, it was me. Which is funny because I was always the one who had it together. The proverbial duck paddling its feet in a panic below the surface while never giving away anything up top. I had become so good at it I had myself fooled.

MEOW!

Mando sits on the floor next to the bed and I let my hand fall to scratch his ear. His purr is instant, and he stretches his paws up on the side of the bed.

Scooting back to make room, I pat the edge of the bed gently.

He pounces with a graceful leap and immediately licks my nose and flicks his tail in my face as he tries to get comfortable. His purr rumbles so loud I wonder if River feels the vibrations through the mattress. I don't think Mando would disapprove of anyone I brought home, but he took to River right away. Part of it could be because River brought him treats that first week, but it was important to me to make sure Mando was okay with a new person around before I asked him to move in.

Thankfully cats don't form real words, but the way he snuggled with River and woke him up just as often as he woke me made me comfortable about it. How ridiculous I felt initially to make sure my cat approved of my life partner before I made any serious moves vanished when I mentioned it to River's dad. He simply patted me on the knee and said it's not wrong to consider a family member's feelings when you want to make big changes in their life. I assured Ray there was no way I was interfering with anything he and River had, but he simply shook his head and told me I could never interfere and he was more than happy to see River find a more meaningful life and someone to share it with.

Ray was the biggest supporter for me to ask River to move in. He was already like a father to me and we'd barely just begun our time together. Another gift River gave me that's priceless.

A hand on my back has me turn my head to find River's sleepy eyes and adorable smile.

"Did I wake you?"

"No, I've been awake for a while. Just drifting in and out."

"Everythin' okay?"

"Could only be better if my man slid over and gave me a kiss."

Rolling away carefully from Mando, I slide over closer to River on his side of the bed. With my hand on his chest, I press my lips to his and laugh when he chases after me for more, as I try to pull away.

"You want more than a kiss, I think."

Shifting so I can cover his body with mine, I stare into his kind eyes.

"A thousand lifetimes wouldn't give me as much as I want with you, Blaze. I want everything. I want your bad moods when stock prices fall and I want your complaining when you eat too much popcorn when we watch movies. I want your joy when you make a difference in an animal's life, and I want your smile when you have your first cup of coffee in the morning."

He cups my cheek in his hand as I listen to his words that stick to my heart like glue and make my eyes water.

"And I want to be in this bed every night with you and wake up every morning. Morning breath and farts under the covers included."

"Hey! That's not very nice!" But my whole body shakes with laughter as I collapse on him. "You ruined a perfectly sweet and romantic moment."

"Did I?"

Kissing his nose, I laugh again.

"No, not really. But... thank you. Because I want all that too."

Our kisses escalate into more and River flips me over on my back. Mando chirps with an evil eye in our direction because we dared jostle him too much.

"Is it weird to have sex with the cat on the bed?"

"I'm fine if you are. It's not like he's going to join in."

"As long as he doesn't watch. That might freak me out a little. It's like a kid in the room."

River goes back to kissing my neck, and I push at him to stop. "What?"

"I have to put Mando out of the room. Now that you compared him to a kid watchin', it's all I'm thinkin' about, and that's gross. What if he's traumatized?"

River rolls off me with a laugh and I scoop up an unhappy Mando. I speed walk to the livingroom and place him on the couch in his favourite spot.

"Sorry buddy, but I'll make it up to you later."

When I return to the bedroom, River has the covers flipped off him and I stumble at the vision of him.

"God, you're beautiful."

There's enough ambient light in the room for me to see all of River, like some kind of otherworldly being who just showed up in my bed. His hand slides down his chest, through his fuzzy belly hair, and grips his plumping cock.

"Wanna get back to what we started? Or are you just gonna watch me?"

Shaking my head, I crawl up the bed and replace his hand with mine while kneeling between his legs. "I want to finish what we started, but not too fast."

He moans with my strokes, and his cock grows in my hand. His lips part as he gasps and watches me as I slowly jerk him off.

"Come up here. I want to do the same to you."

Reluctantly, I let go and slide up next to him after snagging the lube off the nightstand.

"Yesss... " I hiss as his tongue lingers on my hardened nipple and his lips smile against my skin.

River's hands on me are divine, but his mouth is pure sin.

"Your tongue is my undoin', Riv. Fuck...,"

"You're mine. Everything about you ties me in knots. All good ones, though."

I settle next to him and let our mouths collide. Lazy kisses filled with desire and exploring hands roam each other's bodies, grounding us to the moment.

Slippery hands wrap around each other's dick and the delicious, slow slides draw all the air from my lungs.

River wiggles closer and places my hand around both of us. "You take over this part. I want to be in you when you come."

His words are hot and needy over my ear, and I adjust my leg to give him more room. His slippery fingers circle my hole, and my grip on our cocks falters as he slides his fingers inside.

"Oh god... "

I can't decide what I want more, to thrust against his dick or grind down on his fingers. His wicked laugh in my ear tells me he knows my dilemma.

"What do you want, Blaze? Want my dick in you instead? Or do you want to stay like this and come all over me?"

His fingers search and find my sweet spot, bringing me so close to orgasm I can barely speak. He turns me inside out every time we're together, no matter what he does.

"Like this." I pant.

His lips find mine and he fingers me harder. "Lemme feel it Blaze. Come all over my dick with my fingers in you."

I press my mouth to his in a silent scream as the lightning bolt of pleasure shoots through me. Somehow I keep my hand moving as the cum overflows my grip and River presses into my hand.

"Holy shit... " He comes with the sexiest moan I've heard from him, adding to the mess I made in my hand. I spread our mixed release over his stomach and lay soft kisses on his collarbone.

"How... does this... keep getting hotter?" He mumbles between kisses.

"Soul mates or somethin' as equally cheesy?" I offer with a smile against his skin.

But he kisses me with such tenderness it's nothing close to being cheesy.

"Something like that."

EPILOGUE

River

MAY

The cement truck rumbles away and I'm left standing with Blaze staring at the giant slab where my workshop will be built next week.

In the end, I decided it would better serve the old house having the workshop stay on the property. Mom wouldn't have wanted me to be attached to four walls. She wanted me attached to the wood working itself. I have the tools she paid for and the original work I made for her. That's what will make this my shop again and still keep her memory near.

But packing up my stuff for a few weeks while we get everything sorted was a bit of a nightmare. Even living with Blaze for the past few months, I set up a little place in his garage where I could go on those nights insomnia hit. The strange thing, though, is that those nights are very few now. I have a sneaking suspicion it's connected to the man standing next to me.

"Are you still okay with your decision?"

"I'm more than okay, Blaze. My mom would have loved you. This feels more like something she'd be happy to see me do."

My gaze shifts to the new signpost at the end of the driveway. Empty right now but soon it won't be. River Works Custom Carvings will be ready to open in another few months.

"I'm going to miss havin' you at the ranch all the time."

"You're just going to miss grabbing my ass at every spare moment. You'll probably get more done without me."

He gathers me in his arms and I rest my head on his shoulder.

"I might get less done. Dan will be bitchin' at me to stop moonin' over ya and get somethin' done. The other guys will stay out of my way because they don't want to hear me whinin' about it. It'll be rough."

"I'm fifteen minutes down the road. You can come home for lunch if you miss me that much."

His smile fills his face. "I love hearin' you say that."

"Which part?"

"Me comin' home to you."

"Yeah, me too. If it wasn't for you, I never would've got the chance to try the business idea out. I can't thank you enough for that."

"You thank me every time you slide the key in the lock and hang your hat at the door. That's all I need."

He pecks a kiss to my lips and takes me by the hand. "I have a surprise for you, though."

Blaze tugs me along and I don't know what else he could have in store for me. When we first started dating, he said he wanted to be romanced and take it slow and here we are living together less than a year later. Not exactly a slow start, but I'm not complaining. Because I still do the romance bit. I always will because Blaze turns me into this soppy, smooshy man. Not that I was ever a mean person, but he just makes me want to spoil him all the time.

Spoiling a billionaire is easy when you know the way to their heart. He may have a lot of money, but I'm rich with romantic ideas and that pays off for me... very well.

He leads me into the kitchen and on the island is a wrapped box with a bow. It's the kind of box you just lift off the lid and I send him a questioning gaze.

"Open it."

Lifting the lid, I move the tissue paper out of the way and lift out the carving inside.

"You bought this? From the auction?"

"Sort of?"

"Well, I'm sure you didn't steal it. I could've made you one. You didn't have to buy this one."

Placing one of my most favourite creations on the counter, I kiss him thank you.

"Well, I could make a larger donation this way to buy it. That's the first point. And... it's beautiful and from the heart. To me, those faces and that heart captured what my life was like before I met you. Everything was faceless, but not in the way you meant in the carvin'. To me, it was a sign of hope that I could find answers to what I was lookin' for when I came here. To put a face to love. And I did."

"Wow, I'm flattered and I.... that's amazing to hear Blaze."

"I didn't know what to do with it, though, at first. But I think I'd like you to put it in your shop. It's not a carvin' to remind you of anythin' in particular but maybe a reminder that there's someone out there for everyone. And well, you're my someone."

"You're definitely my someone, Blaze."

MEOW

Mando sits at my feet with an indignant cat stare.

"You're my four-legged someone and you come with your dad. I'm not leaving anyone out. Don't worry."

I scoop him up and kiss him on the head, much like Blaze does every time he comes home.

Blaze cocks his head with a loopy smile and I nearly drop Mando with the words that come out of his mouth.

"Marry me."

"What!?"

"Be my husband. Take my name. Be a cat dad with me. Hell, be a real dad with me." He steps forward and cups my face in his hands. "I've been thinkin' of it for a while and just seein' you with my cat and this whole thing with the shop and your shoes by the door. Your coffee mug on the counter and your razor on the sink. I just... marry me, River."

Well if this day could get anymore weird and wonderful, I don't know how.

"Is this how we end our book, then?"

My shaking hands take his in mine.

"Our book is just beginnin' Riv. We have a whole series to write. Don't leave me hangin'."

"If you thought I'd ever say no to marrying you, you're out of your ever loving mind. Yes. Yes, I'll marry you and take your name. I'll be a cat dad, real dad, bringer of coffee and... whatever the hell else you want me to do."

"I guess we're gettin' married."

His crooked smile, so happy and full of love for me, just about does me in. How the hell did I get this lucky?

"I guess we are. Want to go tell my dad?"

"Oh. Should I have asked him first?"

"Proposed to my dad? He'd have said no."

I snort, and he smacks me in the arm. "Jackass. Why do you always have to ruin a moment?"

"Did I?"

I bat my eyelashes at him, and he shakes his head.

"I wouldn't have it any other way, Riv. Let's go see your dad."

I hope you enjoyed Blaze! He was such a joy to write!

Alec is up next!
Or read book one, Colby.
Or if you'd like to visit the Fall Fling again, Take Shelter with Me is Jake's story.

Acknowledgments

I hope you enjoyed Blaze and River just as much as I did writing them. These two were hard to get started initially, but once I just let Blaze talk and do his thing, well, things went a lot smoother after that. At no point was Blaze every planned to propose, it just happened. That should tell you how much I let him get away with things!

As usual, there's people to thank for helping get this book out there.

Janet H and Sarah C, thank you for the honesty. You help me bring a better book to market and I'm very grateful for that.

Janet, you also deserve a special medal for your efforts with this release and all my rambling messages. You made my life so much easier with your help, and I'm forever thankful.

My ARC team, both new and old, thank you from the bottom of my bottom! It's bigger than my heart, haha. Your praise and help with spreading the word is so appreciated. Some days I have to pinch myself when I see people raving about something I wrote. You continue to amaze me with the kind words. Thank you so much for everything you do for me.

To the friends who have listened to me bitch about this book, you're amazing. Thank you for all the ears and encouraging words. You kept me going when I needed it most.

To you, dear reader, the biggest of thanks! Without you, there is no story. Full stop. Thank you for your support.

Until we meet again between the pages,

RM

ALSO BY

www.ingramcontent.com/pod-product-compliance
Lightning Source LLC
Chambersburg PA
CBHW061200210726
48294CB00006B/1702